PURRFECT SPY

THE MYSTERIES OF MAX 88

NIC SAINT

PURRFECT SPY

The Mysteries of Max 88

Copyright © 2024 by Nic Saint

All rights reserved. No part of this book may be reproduced in any form by any electronic or mechanical means including photocopying, recording, or information storage and retrieval without permission in writing from the author.

This is a work of fiction. Names, characters, places, brands, media, and incidents are either the product of the author's imagination or are used fictitiously. The author acknowledges the trademarked status and trademark owners of various products referenced in this work of fiction, which have been used without permission. The publication/use of these trademarks is not authorized, associated with, or sponsored by the trademark owners.

Edited by Chereese Graves

www.nicsaint.com

Give feedback on the book at: info@nicsaint.com

facebook.com/nicsaintauthor
@nicsaintauthor

First Edition

Printed in the U.S.A

PURRFECT SPY

The world's flyest fly is back!

When an actual prince was found murdered at the Star Hotel, we were called in to investigate. It was the start of a very challenging twenty-four hours, with a drive-by shooting following on the heels of the events at the hotel, our friend Harriet being poisoned, trouble brewing at the General Store and Gran launching a new business venture that would make her a billionaire. I had a hard time keeping my wits about me and figuring out what was going on. Fortunately for us, an old friend decided to pitch in: none other than Norm the spying fly.

CHAPTER 1

Carlos Perks stepped out of his car and glanced down at his right foot. He cursed when he saw that he had stepped in a pile of dog poo. At least he thought it was dog poo. It could have been human excrement, since it was a pretty big pile, and no dog he knew produced so much of the stuff, even the big dogs.

He sighed deeply and tried scraping it off the sole of his shoe. He had a big and important business meeting scheduled and he didn't want to be late. But neither did he want to walk into the meeting and soil the hotel carpet with a bunch of smelly stuff. It was a matter of respect for the cleaning crew who would have to shampoo the carpet after he had been through.

A woman walked up to him and touched his arm. He looked up in surprise, but then he saw that it was his fiancée, Mindy.

"I hate it when this happens," he grumbled. "Don't you?"

"I always make sure I look where I walk," she reminded him tartly. He didn't like it when she made these cracks, making him feel stupid. But then it was par for the course with Mindy. She did it with everyone she met, and by now it had become a habit that was hard to break.

"Must have been a big dog," he commented as he glanced around for the culprit. He saw an elderly man walking his dog a little further down the street, but that dog was tiny and couldn't possibly be responsible for the smear of doo-doo left on his shoe.

Mindy was checking her watch and making impatient noises. "Let's go, Carlos," she said. "We don't want to be late for this meeting."

She was right. It was a make-or-break meeting for their business. If they didn't manage to convince the client to put down a big order, they might as well pack up and leave. After all, they had been in business long enough to know that you can't force fate. You can try and make it go your way by making sure that all the elements are in place, but even then it's impossible to predict an outcome. Especially in a business as fickle as the one he and Mindy were in. They had recently expanded their product portfolio to pet food and needed the capital to expand.

He gave his shoe one final scrub against the side of the pavement and then hurried after his fiancée, who was already setting a nervous pace in the direction of the entrance to the Star Hotel, where their client would hopefully be in a good mood—a spending mood. Bug spray had been done before, but their particular product was definitely very novel and could set the market on fire if they ended up bagging just another couple of big orders. Even though Prince Abdullah was a repeat customer that didn't mean they didn't have to fight for his business.

He hoisted his mock-up, up in his arms. The giant fly, which he had christened Virgil, never failed to impress, especially when combined with the PowerPoint presentation he had designed. As he lugged the giant thing into the hotel, he drew plenty of surprised and amused looks from the people in the lobby, who probably had never seen a man carry a giant fly in his arms before. Virgil was also the mascot of their company, which they had named Zap, Inc.

"Come on, come *on*," Mindy urged as she pressed the elevator call button. The meeting wasn't taking place in one of the conference rooms but in the client's suite for some reason.

They arrived on the third floor, and Mindy traced a path to the door of the suite in question with her high-heeled Louboutins. If Prince Abdullah took one look at Mindy and liked what he saw, he might part with his money for the simple pleasure of being in the woman's presence. He wouldn't be the first man to fall for the peppy blonde and certainly not the last.

They paused in front of the designated door, and Mindy gave him a critical look. Then she got busy making sure that his hair looked just so, his shirt was buttoned up, his tie straight and his shoes spic and span.

"You need a personal stylist," she said finally as she threw up her hands.

"I *have* a personal stylist," he reminded her. "You!"

She half-smiled at this. "Funny guy." She turned serious. "Let's knock 'em dead, Carlos."

"Yeah, let's," he agreed. He applied his knuckles to the door, and they waited for Aladdin's cave to open and shower them with lots and lots of money to make their dreams come true.

When after ten seconds there was no answer, he knocked again. And when there still was no sign that anyone was home, he exchanged a look of concern with his fiancée.

"Maybe he forgot?" he suggested.

"Impossible," she said as she took out her phone. "He confirmed the meeting this morning."

He hesitated. "Maybe he's in the shower?"

"Let me try," she said, and hit the door with her fist. The door rattled on its hinges since Mindy was a strong girl who loved her daily gym class and could bench press more than Carlos. He had never been one for physical exertion, preferring to spend his time on his creations. Like the innovative and revolutionary bug spray he had invented all by himself. Or the giant fly he was still holding in his arms. The creature seemed to be staring at him with its huge facet eyes, and even he got a little anxious when he looked into the big fly's eyes. You could be forgiven for thinking it was real, even though it was all polyester and styrofoam.

"I hope he hasn't changed his mind," said Carlos. "We need this sale, sweetheart."

"I know we need this sale," she said annoyedly. "I'll send him another message."

She expertly and quickly typed out the message on her phone. Her fingers flew over the screen at a dizzying speed. Moments later, the message was sent and she was frowning at the device. "He's received it, but he hasn't seen it yet," she announced. Then ten seconds later, "He still hasn't seen it." She lifted her eyes to take in his. He saw that she was starting to get seriously rattled now, which wasn't like her. "Something is wrong, Carlos. Very wrong."

"Maybe the prince changed his mind?" he suggested.

"But why? Half an hour ago everything was fine, so what changed?"

He shrugged. But since he was essentially a philosopher at heart, he didn't think there was a lot they could do right now except accept their loss and go home. There would be other clients since essentially they had an excellent product to sell. Though Prince Abdullah represented their big break. If not for him, they'd never have cracked the Asian market in the first place.

Suddenly there was a sort of commotion on the other side of the door, and he placed his ear to the panel. "Did you hear that?"

"What?"

"Sounded like… a gurgle or something?"

"What gurgle? I didn't hear anything."

The sound had died away, but he had definitely heard it. He wore pretty high prescription glasses, and he'd once read that if you lose one of your senses, the others are all augmented, so his hearing was excellent and a lot better than Mindy's, who never seemed to hear anything.

"There's definitely somebody in there," he said.

"Of course there's somebody in there," said Mindy. "Only he doesn't want to see us, does he? Must have had a change of heart, just like you said. Come on. Let's go. I'm starting to feel like a fool, and I hate it when that happens."

And she started to walk away, with that same brisk pace that was so typical for her. But the gurgle had given Carlos pause. Was it possible that the prince was in some kind of trouble?

And so he decided to give it one final shot. He put his fist to the door and gave it a vigorous rap. And much to his surprise, he thought he could detect another gurgle. And so without thinking, he set down the mock-up of Virgil and put his shoulder to the door.

"What do you think you're doing?" asked Mindy, who had retraced her steps.

"There's someone in trouble in there!" he said, and took a step back, then assaulted the door once again, this time throwing all of his not inconsiderable weight into it. The door buckled under the pressure, and he flew inside, landing on the carpeted floor, right next to a person.

As he stared at the man, he found himself looking straight into the eyes of Prince Abdullah himself. And in spite of the earlier gurgling, it was undeniable that life was now extinct!

CHAPTER 2

I had been watching a little bird tweeting up a storm in a nearby tree when a voice rang out inside the house.

"Max! Dooley!"

I exchanged a look of understanding with my friend Dooley, who was studying an ant crawling over a blade of grass and trying its darndest to carry a large crumb to safety.

"Looks like it's time for us to get off our butts and do some real work for a change, buddy," I told him.

"Pity. I was just about to help this little fella here feed his family." He sighed. "I'm sorry, little ant. Looks like you'll have to carry that crumb over the hill to your nest all by yourself."

"Who are you talking to?" asked Brutus, who had been sunning himself and lying on his back, all four paws dangling this way and that.

"A little ant," Dooley explained. "He's carrying a big load, and I wanted to help him out."

"What's going on?" asked Harriet, emerging from a nearby bush. "What's with all the yelling and screaming?"

"The yelling and the screaming was Odelia," I said. "Who probably has some new case she wants us to assist her on."

"Dooley can't assist her today," said Brutus. "On account of the fact that he needs to help a little old ant cross the road." He grinned and gave me a wink.

I rolled my eyes. Brutus has a habit of teasing Dooley from time to time, even though Dooley is probably the sweetest cat in the world. But then again, maybe that's why he attracts Brutus's mockery. It's always the best ones who get scorn piled on top of their heads, isn't it?

"I think Dooley is doing a great job," I said. "Keep up the good work, buddy."

"Thanks, Max," said Dooley, pleased by this endorsement.

"Oh, please," said Brutus. "If every ant needed the assistance of a cat they'd get lazy and would stop building their nests for themselves. It's exactly this kind of struggle and strife that builds character, Max." He balled a fist and shook it. "It builds backbone. So taking that away from your little old ant is doing it a disservice. It's crippling him and making sure he won't be able to get through life and challenge its hurdles and vicissitudes."

"Gee," said Dooley. "I didn't think about it that way, Brutus. But I guess you're right. I shouldn't help this little ant but encourage it to carry its load all by itself." He lowered his face to the ant. "I'm sorry, Mr. Ant. Looks like you're on your own. But not to worry. Brutus says it will build character and give you backbone." He gave me a questioning look. "Do ants even have a backbone, Max? Do they have a spine?"

"I'm not sure," I said. My knowledge of ants is very sketchy, I have to admit.

"Okay, I'm not telling you again," said Odelia, suddenly busting through the kitchen door and walking out into the backyard. She stood there, her fists planted on her hips.

"Lazy bunch," she said, but she smiled as she said it, which softened the blow her words caused.

"I'll have you know I'm not lazy!" said Harriet. "I've been thinking very hard about my next project, which is going to bring us all a lot of money, so that's time well spent, wouldn't you say?"

"And what project would that be?" asked Odelia.

"Too soon to tell," said Harriet. "That's why I was thinking so hard."

"And what about you, Brutus?" asked our human. "What were you doing?"

"I was, um… also thinking hard," said the big black cat. "In sync with Harriet, you know."

"Thinking about the same project, huh? What about you, Max?"

"I was looking at a bird," I said truthfully. I didn't see a reason to lie about being lazy. After all, some of the greatest minds claim that being lazy causes fresh thoughts to pop into one's head, and the best ideas come from their inventors being lazy and doing nothing.

"And you, Dooley?" asked Odelia.

"I was thinking about helping this ant," said Dooley. "But Brutus said I shouldn't, since it has to carry its burden all by itself, so it can build a backbone and deal with vivid tunes."

"Vicissitudes," Brutus corrected him.

Odelia's smile widened. "Okay, what I wanted to ask you is this: do you think you'll be able to drag yourselves away from your busy lives to assist me in a new investigation?"

"What investigation?" asked Harriet.

"A prince has been murdered at the Star Hotel," said Odelia. "And hotel management has called it in. So Chase and I are going over there to take a closer look at what's going on."

"A prince has been murdered?" asked Harriet, her eyes

sparkling. "Now that I have to see. I love princes," she confessed. "They're rich and handsome."

"Not this one," said Odelia. "This one is dead."

"Doesn't matter," said Harriet. "Princes always travel in packs. Where there's one there are bound to be others."

"Okay, so let's go," said Odelia, as she clapped her hands. "You know the drill. Talk to any and all pet witnesses you can find, and extract as much information from them as you can."

She certainly made it sound easy, but I know from experience that some of these pets don't want to talk to a couple of cats, others are too traumatized by the death of their humans to collect their thoughts and say anything useful, and still others are downright hostile and a menace to any cat with a healthy sense of self-preservation, which I pride myself to possess.

But since Odelia is the boss and we are her loyal pets, we did as she asked and abandoned our respective positions on the lawn to traipse after her. Moments later, we were en route to the downtown area where the Star Hotel is located. A boutique hotel that caters to a wealthy clientele, it sets the standard for any hotels eager to supply excellence of service to its guests. I've never actually stayed there, but I've been there plenty of times, as it seems to attract both the upscale clientele I mentioned but also the criminal element eager to prey on that same clientele. I guess wealth inspires envy and covetousness in people who don't want to work for a living but simply relieve those who do of their hard-earned personal possessions.

We arrived at the hotel to see several police vehicles parked in front of the building. Kingman, whose owner runs the General Store, was looking at us from across the street, and so we waved at him. "Remind me to talk to Kingman when we're done here," I told Dooley.

"But why, Max? Do you think he has seen what happened?"

I shrugged. "He's a potential witness, that's all."

Since Kingman likes to sit in front of the General Store, which is located directly across the street from the hotel, there's always a chance he might have seen something—or someone.

"The killer won't have come crawling out of the window, if that's what you're suggesting, Max," said Brutus, who was in one of his vitriolic and acerbic moods today I noticed.

"He could have passed *by* the window," I said. Many a killer will pass in front of the window of the room he has selected to satiate those murderous urges and will be seen from across the street. Though Brutus was right in suggesting that it was a long shot.

The elevator took us up to the third floor, where plenty of police activity was already taking place, with officers talking to any and all neighbors of the guest who had been killed. Before long, we arrived at the room in question, and when we entered, immediately came upon the dead person, who was lying just beyond the door, in the entrance hall.

Abe Cornwall, the county coroner, was crouched next to the man, studying him intently, trying to ascertain what had made him the way he was. The victim was a swarthy individual, I saw, and dressed in uncommon garb: a long flowing white robe and also a headdress that I hadn't seen very often on the streets of Hampton Cove. He also had a perfectly coiffed little black beard that must have cost him plenty of time in the morning to make look just right. He was quite young, I thought. Late twenties maybe, or early thirties. Handsome, too.

"Looks like he was killed by two gunshot wounds to the chest," said Abe as he pointed to two bloodied spots on the white robe. "This second one will probably be what killed him. It still took him a while to die, though, according to the couple who found him." He looked up with a sparkle in his eyes. "He was still gurgling when they found him. Gurgling, Chase." He pointed to the man's face. "See the blood on his lips? Poor guy tried to call out for help."

Chase made a face. "Caliber?" the detective asked curtly.

"I'll know more when I dig out the slugs. But it's a small caliber weapon."

"Handgun?"

"Looks like it. But like I said, I'll know more once I get this fella on my slab."

"Who found him?" asked Odelia.

"A couple selling bug spray," said Chase. "They were expecting a sales presentation and instead walked in on this. They're in the room across the hall, waiting to be interviewed."

"Bug spray?" asked Abe with a grin as he got up to his feet. "I didn't know the good people from Abou-Yamen were in the market for bug spray. It's just a lot of desert over there, right?"

"Even in the desert there are bugs, Abe," said Chase. "There are bugs everywhere."

"I've never been to Abou-Yamen, I'm sorry to say," said Abe as he peeled off his plastic gloves. "From what I've heard it's a beautiful country. And the climate is perfect, of course."

"Too hot for my taste," said Chase. "But then I've never liked the heat." He glanced down at the victim. "But you're right. It is a little odd that a prince from the kingdom of Abou-Yamen would meet with a couple of bug spray salespeople in a hotel room in Hampton Cove."

"And be murdered for his trouble," said Abe. He smiled. "One thing I can tell you right now, it wasn't bug spray that killed him." He gave Chase and Odelia a two-fingered salute. "I'll have my report on your boss's desk at my earliest possible convenience. Feel free to peruse it to your heart's content. I find that it makes for excellent reading. But then I guess I'm biased."

Odelia and Chase watched him walk away. "An artist who loves his own work," said Odelia. "You have to admit it's admirable."

"That's one way of putting it," said Chase. He gestured to the door. "Interview the witnesses, spouse?"

"Lead the way, spouse."

CHAPTER 3

We found our two witnesses in the room across the corridor, as promised, and it was true that they looked discombobulated, but then I guess most people would feel this way when they come across a dead body. It's one thing to see it in the movies or read about it, and quite a different experience altogether to encounter it in real life. Both of the people we saw looked extremely pale, with the woman looking as if she was about to throw up—or perhaps she already had.

In a corner of the room, I saw a large mock-up of a fly, and it immediately attracted my attention. It isn't every day that you see a fly blown up to such proportions, and I immediately made a beeline for the bug. As mock-ups go, it was extremely well done and looked very real.

"This is amazing, Max," said Dooley. "It looks like a real fly—only ten times bigger."

"How about a million times bigger?" said Brutus as he studied the bug from every angle.

"I think it looks scary," said Harriet. "Imagine if this was an actual fly. It would wreak havoc on our town, you guys.

It would be like a horror movie! It would be fly armageddon!"

"It's not a real fly," I said. "It's just plastic and rubber and foam with a lick of paint. Though it's true that it's extremely well done. Whoever made this is an artist in their own right."

"I made it," said the artist in question. "It was for my presentation to Prince Abdullah. We've developed a new type of bug spray, a much improved version of our old one, and I decided to bring along this fly to add a little oomph to my sales pitch. These things tend to be very dry, and so I thought that some didactic material would help get our message across."

"And that message is?" asked Chase, who was busy taking notes, but couldn't help darting an occasional look at the fly, which was a real eye-catcher.

"Our bug spray is one hundred percent environmentally friendly," said the man, whose name was Carlos Perks and who was a chemist. "Most insecticides are very harmful to the environment, and so they should be used with extreme caution. My bug spray is perfectly safe. It can even be inhaled or ingested by a person and they won't experience any adverse effects."

"And still one hundred percent effective in eradicating the pests," said his fiancée, whose name was Mindy Horsefield. The woman was making a superhuman effort to engage herself in conversation, but it was clear to all present that she was having a pretty hard time at it.

"Maybe you should lie down, Ms. Horsefield," Odelia suggested. "We can do this interview at a later time."

"No, let's do it now," she said adamantly. "Better to get it over with."

"So can you tell us in your own words what happened when you arrived at Prince Abdullah's room?" asked Chase.

"Well, I knocked," said Mindy. "And when there was no

answer, I knocked again. And then, just when we were about to go, Carlos thought he heard a sound coming from the room."

"What kind of sound?" asked Odelia.

"Like a gurgle?" said Carlos. "Or maybe a groan or something? It's just that we thought that maybe the prince had forgotten about our meeting."

"Even though he had texted me only half an hour before that the meeting was definitely a go," said Mindy with a shrug. "So I knew that he must have changed his mind."

"But then you heard this gurgle or groan," Odelia prompted.

Carlos nodded. "That's right. It seemed to come from inside the room, and so I decided that maybe the prince was in some kind of trouble. And that maybe we should get in there."

"And then you broke down the door," said Chase dryly.

Carlos gave him a nervous look. "I'll pay for the damage, of course."

"Nonsense," said Mindy. "You acted on impulse. The impulse to save a life. And turns out you were right. Someone attacked the prince. Only we were too late to save him."

"Is he…" Carlos gulped and I could see his Adam's apple jumping up and down. "Is he dead?"

"I'm afraid so, sir," said Odelia. "He was shot."

"Shot!" said Mindy. "Oh, my God!"

"You didn't hear a gunshot?" asked Chase.

Both Carlos and Mindy shook their heads. "Like I said, all I heard was some kind of strange gurgle coming from inside the room," said Carlos. "I wasn't sure what it meant but I got this sudden feeling that something was seriously wrong, and that maybe I should do something."

"If it had been up to me I would have gone down to

reception," said Mindy. "But Carlos figured he couldn't wait that long. So he burst into that room and…" She grimaced and her face went a shade paler than it had already been. "And then we saw…" She closed her eyes.

"I fell to the floor and came face to face with the prince," said Carlos softly as he stared before him and wrung his hands. "He was just lying there, looking at me. Eyes wide open."

"I knew the moment I laid eyes on the prince that he was dead," said Mindy. "He had that look in his eyes, you know. A look of terror. Like you see in the movies sometimes."

"Was there anyone else in the room apart from Prince Abdullah?" asked Chase.

Mindy shook her head. But then she slung a hand to her face. "Oh, my God. You mean, the killer?! You think he was still in there?" She turned to Carlos. "He could have shot us, too!"

"I don't think he was in there," said Carlos. "If he was, we would have seen him."

"He was probably hiding," said Mindy. She turned to Chase. "Was he there, you think?"

"I'm sorry, but at this moment we have no way of knowing," said Chase.

"But… is there another exit?"

"There's the balcony," said Chase. "Most likely he got out that way."

Mindy looked sick now. "I'm sorry, but I need to…" And suddenly she bolted in the direction of the bathroom, slammed the door, and a moment later we could hear the telltale sounds of a person relieving themselves of the remnants of their breakfast.

"Apologies for my fiancée," said Carlos. "It's the first time that she… that we… I mean, we've never…" He swallowed with some difficulty, and I got the impression that he would soon be joining Mindy in that bathroom.

"Let's go and find us some witnesses of our own," Brutus suggested, and darted a final look at the giant fly.

"Too bad it's not a real fly," said Dooley. "I'm sure it would have a great story to tell."

It reminded me that once upon a time we had made the acquaintance of an actual fly, who had done some great work for us. The thing is that cats are great spies, but even they can't beat a fly, since they can get into any room and simply spend time there, unobserved by anyone. The proverbial fly on the wall, in other words, but then for real.

Dooley must have also remembered our friendly spying fly, for the moment Harriet and Brutus had left the room, he said, "I wonder who Carlos used as a model to create this, Max. Do you think it was our friend Norm?"

I smiled. "I'm sure he didn't need to use a model, Dooley," I said. "He probably found a picture of a fly online and used it to create this mock-up."

"I wish Norm was here now," said Dooley. "I wonder what he would think about this mock-up. Like looking in a mirror, I imagine. Only one of those funny mirrors at the playground that make you look ten times your own size."

And just when we were about to leave the room to look for those pet witnesses Odelia had mentioned, a fly flew in through the open window and settled on the wall next to the giant mock-up. And as it took in its likeness in polystyrene, it seemed not to like what it saw, for suddenly it burst out, "That is not how I look!"

Dooley gaped at the fly. "Norm, is that you?" he asked.

The fly seemed to notice us for the first time, for suddenly he cried, "Dooley! Max! Oh, it's so great to see you guys!"

I would have said that a lot of hugging and backslapping

followed, but unfortunately, flies are too small—or cats too big—to engage in that kind of friendly interaction. So instead, we simply sufficed by taking up position closer to our friend and expressing our surprise that we had just been talking about him and all of a sudden there he was.

"It's such a pity to see you!" said Dooley.

"You mean serendipity," I corrected him.

"That, too!" Dooley cried, happy to see our friend.

Over the course of our investigations, we've made so many great friends and met so many pets and other creatures that it's always fun to see them again. And since once again we were faced with a mystery, Norm had arrived just in time.

"What are you guys doing here?" he asked. "Except looking at this abomination, of course."

"It belongs to that guy over there," said Dooley, pointing to Carlos. "He has designed a bug spray that is lethal to bugs but safe for humans and pets, and so he wanted to demonstrate it to a potential client by using it on this mock-up fly."

"I don't think he was actually going to try and kill the mock-up fly," I told him. "Since it isn't a real fly, you see."

"Of course it's not a real fly," said Norm. "It doesn't even look like a fly!"

It certainly looked like a fly to me, but then what do I know? It's like being a dog and figuring all cats look the same, and vice versa. I guess it's the same with flies. To me, all flies look the same, even though they're probably all different.

"A man was murdered," I said in answer to Norm's question. "And so it's up to us to find out what happened." I gave him a curious look. "You wouldn't have a moment to spare, would you?"

"I thought you'd never ask. A nice murder mystery is just what I need. To take my mind off things, I mean."

I was afraid to ask but did so anyway. "Take your mind off what things, Norm?"

"Trouble with the missus," he said.

"I didn't know you were married?"

"Oh, I am. Only now it looks as if I won't be married much longer. It all started when I refused to condone her desire to start a family, you see."

"You don't want to start a family?"

"Of course not! I mean, fathering hundreds of kids? Who has the time? I've got my own ambitions. And you know what it's like: the moment you start a family, you're trapped. Trapped in the kind of drudgery that is death to a creative and enterprising fly like me. Anyway, when I told her I didn't want kids, she blew her top. I had to get away, so I decided to take a tour around the block. And who would I meet? You guys! I'm telling you, it's kismet!"

It certainly felt like kismet to me, and so we told Norm all about the murder inquiry that we had been tasked with. He immediately agreed to use his unique skill set to get us the information we needed to tackle this mystery. And as he flew off to talk to any witness he could find, we did the same. Without the flying part, that is.

I just hoped that we could put this case to bed real fast, for I was experiencing a pressing and urgent need to return to my backyard and finish doing what I was doing before Odelia came to fetch us, which was exactly nothing.

CHAPTER 4

Rogelio Hartshorn checked his watch, then took a final long drag from his cigarette and threw it on the floor, extinguishing it with the heel of his fine Italian shoe. "What's taking her so long?" he muttered annoyedly. He'd been standing in front of Mitzy's Tea Shoppe for so long he felt as if he was about to become a permanent fixture to this section of Hampton Cove's downtown area. A living statue, in other words, though if it took much longer, he might just as well be a dead statue.

A white van slowed down and he glanced in its direction, hopeful that it would be the woman he'd been waiting for. Her name was Marjorie Collett, and for some reason she had told him to meet outside the tea shop and not in his office, where he mostly met new clients. When the van was almost level with him, a window was lowered and an automatic firearm appeared. And as he stared at the deadly contraption, it started spitting out bullets and hammering his surroundings. As he stood there, too shocked to react, the weapon was quickly withdrawn, the window raised, and the van sped off, with screeching and smoking tires.

For a moment he just stood there, then he checked himself for bullet wounds. He didn't feel any pain, and his corpus seemed fully intact, so he let out a long, shuddering breath of relief.

Several people came hurrying up to him, to see if he was all right. He would have told them he was fine, but for some reason found that in the brief moments that the gun had spat out a series of bullets in his direction, he had lost his capacity for speech. When finally his vocal cords decided to report for duty once more, he breathed, "The police! We have to call the police!"

"Way ahead of you, buddy," said a thickset man as he held up his phone. He then yelled into the device, "Yes, a drive-by shooting! On Grover Street! Better hurry and catch those gangsters!" The moment he had disconnected, he held up his phone once more. "I got the whole thing on my phone," he told a still-stricken Rogelio. "I was filming that cute little statuette over there when this thing went down and so I got it all on film. Wanna see?"

And without waiting for Rogelio's approval, he showed him the video he'd shot of the incident. All Rogelio could think was that he looked very pale and could do with some more time spent outside instead of in his office. The Bahamas, maybe, or Hawaii. The most miraculous thing, though, was that he was fine, even though an attempt had just been made on his life.

"How are you feeling?" asked a woman, giving him a solicitous look as she checked his body for bullet holes. "I don't see anything," she added, and Rogelio couldn't help but notice there was a touch of disappointment in her voice, as if the carnage she had been expecting hadn't been delivered and she personally blamed him for the lack of cooperation.

"I don't think I'm hurt," he announced as he checked the

wall behind him and saw that it was riddled with bullets and had suffered plenty of damage to the brickwork.

"It's almost as if they missed you on purpose," said the man who had shown him the video.

"Impossible," said the woman. "You'd have to be an incredible marksman to shoot around a person in such a way."

"You're probably both right," said a third onlooker. "The AR-15 is a weapon that's known for its accuracy. It's very hard to miss, especially considering they fired off an entire clip."

"Okay, so they were probably incompetent shooters," the woman amended her statement.

"Incompetent or not," said a fourth witness, "you, sir, are one lucky son of a gun."

Rogelio let out a sigh of relief. "Extremely lucky," he agreed.

Just then, a car pulled up at the curb, and a couple of police officers jumped out. One of them made a beeline for him and asked, "Was it you who reported being attacked, sir?"

He nodded, glad that the cavalry had arrived. "That's right."

"I saw the whole thing, officer," said the video man. He swung his phone. "And I've got it all on video. It's right here, from the start to the very shocking end, with our brave hero still standing while all around him devastation was wreaked by that hailstorm of lethal bullets strafing the rustic scene." He grinned and gave Rogelio a wink. "I write crime thrillers as a hobby. And I hope you won't mind, but I think I'll use this in one of my next books."

He nodded, unsure how to respond to this. "Okay, sir, let's get you out of here," said the cop as he started steering him in the direction of the police vehicle.

"I really don't know what happened," he said. "One moment I was standing there, minding my own business, and all of a sudden this van slowed down and they started shooting at me!"

"It's all right here," said the woman as she gestured to the wall that was pockmarked with bullet holes. "There must be at least two dozen bullets that were fired, see? Maybe more."

One of the officers approached the wall and nodded thoughtfully. "It's a miracle you escaped with your life, sir," he said.

In a shaky voice, he admitted, "You can say that again!"

But then he was ushered into the car, and moments later they were mobile. It was only then that he remembered that he'd been waiting for Marjorie Collett to arrive. And as he took out his phone to send her a message he wouldn't be able to honor their meeting, he wondered for the first time why he would have suddenly found himself the victim of an attempt on his life.

CHAPTER 5

Norm was buzzing around the hotel room where the suspects—or rather witnesses—of the murder of the prince were being interviewed. He wondered if he should have taken on the assignment or not. He wanted to help his friends, of course, but as he had told Max and Dooley, he had his own problems to deal with, in the form of some marital strife. Then again, maybe a murder inquiry was exactly what he needed to take his mind off those problems. As he buzzed on, he had a hard time keeping his eyes—all one-thousand-five-hundred facets of them—from taking in that abomination the murderers—or witnesses—had created. Whatever they thought, it looked nothing like a real fly at all. On the contrary, it was a caricature of a fly. What humans thought flies looked like. In other words: it was an insult. A mockery. A travesty! But then what can you expect from people whose life's work it is to murder flies like him.

Bug spray salespeople, Max had called them. No wonder they had finally snapped. It all starts innocently enough, with the odd ant that gets burned under a magnifying glass, then these miscreants move on to pulling off the wings of a fly and finally graduate to creating bug sprays and committing mass murder. Bug genocide, in other words. And when that doesn't satiate their bloodlust, they start killing their own. It was exactly what must have happened here, but since Max was such a big fan of humans, Norm hadn't wanted to give his friend the benefit of his suspicions. Instead, he'd go through the motions and conduct his investigation. It all seemed like a big waste of time, but then of course Max was just like his humans: they all wanted evidence. Well, he'd give them evidence. He'd give them irrefutable evidence!

And so he buzzed from the room and across the corridor, where men and women dressed in white were packing up the body of the dead man and placing him on a stretcher, to be carted off to a place they called the morgue, where a man with frizzy hair would conduct certain experiments and try to determine what made him dead in the first place. Another big waste of time according to Norm, for it was obvious what killed the fella: there were holes in his chest that shouldn't have been there. You can't drill holes in a man's chest and expect him to live.

Humans are fragile, after all, and they don't take holes drilled into the various parts of their anatomy well. In other words: not a very hardy species at all!

He settled on the wall near the crime scene and watched as they packed up the man in a body bag and placed him on the stretcher. He wondered where he would find potential witnesses so he studied the room. As far as he could tell, there were no other flies present, which was a pity, for they could have provided him with the evidence he needed. But as he looked closer, he detected a friendly face poking its head out from under the bed. So he immediately flew down from his perch on the wall and took up position next to his old friend Bill.

"Hey, buddy," he said, happy to meet another friend. After

Max and Dooley, this was the third friend he'd met in a short time and it lifted his troubled heart. "How are things?"

"Can't complain," said Bill, giving him the kind of hangdog look that was a hallmark of his personality. Being a cockroach, Bill had witnessed his fair share of crime scenes over the course of a long life, and had taken part in the removal of plenty of corpses, so Norm sincerely hoped that he could help him out by providing him with a blow-by-blow account of what had gone down.

"You wouldn't happen to have seen what went down here, would you? It's just that I've been asked to look into this murder business by a couple of good friends of mine, and anything you could tell me would be much appreciated."

Bill hardly seemed interested in what Norm had to say, for he barely looked up at his request. "Hm?" he finally said. "What was that you said, Norm?"

"I said, did you see what happened here? With the dead guy and all?"

"Dead guy?" said Bill, perking up a little. "What dead guy?" Death and decay are very much part of a cockroach's life, and so the fact that he hadn't noticed the presence of a dead body was an oversight that spoke of Bill's preoccupation with other things.

"Is everything all right with you, buddy?" asked Norm. "You look a little peaky."

"It's all right," said Bill. Even his antennae were at half-mast, indicating he had his own cross to bear, not unlike Norm himself. "Trouble with the missus," he explained.

"You don't say," Norm said, marveling at the coincidence.

Bill nodded sadly. "It's her sister Susan, you see. She just lost her husband, and so Melinda insisted she move in with us for the time being. Only me and Susan have never gotten along all that great. And so I told Melinda that I didn't think her sister moving in with us was such a good idea. And so now she's mad at me. Accusing me of bearing a grudge against her family, when it's the other way around. It's Melinda's family who have never taken to me." He sighed deeply. "Never marry, Norm. It's the death by a thousand cuts."

"I *am* married," said Norm. "Though the wife and I are going through a rough patch at the moment." And so he told his friend about Norma's desire to start a family and his reluctance.

"Don't do it," said Bill urgently. "Don't give in, Norm. The moment you have kids, there's no way back."

"No, I guess there isn't," he agreed. "Why, do you have kids?"

"Do I have kids?" said Bill. "Talk about the bane of my existence. All one hundred of them."

Norm swallowed with difficulty. He was glad now that he had met an old friend who had been through the exact same thing he was going through. "But… what do I do?" he asked.

Bill gave him a mournful look. "Just say no, buddy."

Just say no. Was it really that simple? Probably not. If he refused to give Norma what she wanted, she might decide that a divorce was in order. After all, hadn't he promised her to start a family as soon as they were comfortably settled? Only at the time he'd been so over the moon that a gorgeous gal like Norma would be interested in a mere housefly like himself, that he would have promised her the moon and the sky and everything in between.

He gave Bill a grateful look. "Thanks for the advice, buddy," he said, which is when he remembered why he had accosted the cockroach in the first place. "So you didn't notice anything out of the ordinary? One human murdering another by shooting him with a gun?"

Bill sighed unhappily. "Can't say I did. But then I must confess I've been pretty tired these last couple of weeks.

That's the problem with having kids, you know. You're so exhausted all the time that life passes you by." He glanced in the direction of the chalk outline on the floor, where the victim had fallen. "I do seem to remember I heard the sound of raised voices a little while ago. People fighting, you know. I didn't pay them any mind, of course, since humans do that sort of thing all the time. And anyway, who's interested in a couple of humans, unless of course they drop some nice chunk of their breakfast on the carpet, the way this fella did."

"He dropped his breakfast on the floor?"

"He did, yeah. And I can tell you exactly what it was. A tasty piece of buttered toast, with the buttered side hitting the carpet, as it always does, and a piece of pork sausage. Pretty yummy, I have to admit, and always welcome." He slumped a little. "Though it did remind me of Melinda, and how I should probably save some for her, but even if I did, she wouldn't appreciate the gesture, furious as she is over my so-called beef with Susan."

"Susan?"

"The sister. Try to keep up, buddy."

"I'm sorry. Susan, of course. So you were saying the victim dropped his breakfast on the carpet. Anything else that might shed some light on who shot him?"

Bill shook his head slowly. "The strange thing is that I didn't even notice he was dead. I just figured he was taking a nap. Humans do get tired so easily, don't you find? And they can sleep for hours. Really weird."

"I know, right?" said Norm. Then he decided to play his trump card. Since he already knew the killer, he didn't see this as leading the witness. And besides, they weren't in a court of law and he wasn't a prosecutor. Merely an independent investigator brought in by Max and Dooley to assist them so whatever rules they adhered to didn't apply to him.

"Look, I know who did it. There's this couple in the room across the corridor, see, and they've developed a bug spray."

"A bug spray?"

"Yeah, to kill all of us bugs."

Bill made a face. "That's not good."

"No, it sure isn't. They were meeting with the victim. Something about getting him on board as a client. Only there must have been some bad blood between them, because it's my firm belief they are the ones who killed him. I mean, if they're capable of murdering innocent bugs like us, why wouldn't they go the whole hog and murder their fellow man also, right?"

"Absolutely," said Bill. "I like your thinking, Norm."

"So?" he said.

Bill gave him a questioning look. "So what?"

"So did you see them? Shoot the guy, I mean?"

Bill grimaced. "I wish I could say I did, buddy. But like I said, I was so preoccupied with Melinda and her sister that I didn't pay much attention to the guy. I'm sorry."

"That's all right." And so he said his goodbyes to his one and only witness—who hadn't seen anything—and wished him well in his marital strife, and flew off. At least now he knew what the victim had for breakfast. Not that it mattered, but then maybe it did. Max was an ace detective, and so maybe he could deduce from the way the guy buttered his toast, his entire life story and also the way he met his maker.

As he was zooming back to the other room to report back to Max, he was almost swatted by an irate-looking police officer who stood guarding the door. It was a narrow escape, and he was reminded once again what horrible creatures humans are. To try and murder an innocent fly who hasn't done them any harm whatsoever, just because they can. Gah!

CHAPTER 6

Norm had only just flown off, thoroughly excited about the mission we had given him, when there was some kind of altercation on the street below. People were screaming, and when we hurried over to the window to take a look, we saw that the throng of shoppers was heading in the direction of a side street, in anticipation of something that must have taken place there.

"Could be a sale," Harriet suggested. She and Brutus had returned, to announce that they had discovered nothing. "People are always reacting like this when there's a big sale going."

"Or it could be a show," Brutus said. "A busker putting on a great performance."

"Or a celebrity?" Dooley said. "Maybe George Clooney is in town and people are all trying to take a selfie with the man?"

But then Chase's phone rang and it wasn't long before the mystery was solved. "There's been a shooting," he informed Odelia in a low voice, so as not to alarm Carlos and Mindy, who were still seated on the couch, with Mindy still looking very pale and undone.

"A shooting?" asked Odelia. "Here in Hampton Cove?"

The cop nodded. "On Grover Street. Looks like a drive-by shooting. The victim was unharmed—miraculous escape, Dolores said. They're taking him to the hospital just to make sure. She asked us to meet him there."

"But what about the prince?"

"The prince will have to wait," said Chase. "This is more urgent."

I didn't necessarily agree. If Carlos had heard a gurgle or a groan coming from inside the prince's room, that meant that the killer could have been in there with his victim at the time, and that gurgle or groan could have been the prince being shot and trying to cry out for help. So where had the killer gone, if Carlos and Mindy had been standing at the door? One thing was for sure: he or she couldn't have gone far and might still be on the premises, even if he had escaped via the balcony. But since Chase was in charge of the investigation, he called the shots.

"Do we have to go too, Odelia?" asked Dooley.

But she shook her head in a sign that we were to stay put, which I thought was sound thinking on her part. If the crowd moving in the direction of Grover Street was anything to go on, this second crime scene would be pretty crowded by now, and a couple of cats might get trampled underfoot if that was the case.

"We'll keep looking for witnesses," I assured our human, and she gave me a grateful pat on the head.

An officer was charged to keep an eye on Carlos and Mindy, and in the meantime, the investigation would continue, with officers knocking on doors of the adjacent rooms and asking guests if they had heard or seen anything suspicious.

"We should really look at CCTV footage," said Odelia as she made to follow her husband.

"Way ahead of you, babe," he said. "I've already asked the guy in charge of hotel security to get me that footage ASAP. Right now we have a drive-by shooting to look into."

It certainly was a nice change of pace for the duo, I thought.

"What is a drive-by shooting, Max?" asked Dooley.

"Well, it's a shooting that happens while people are driving by," I said.

He stared at me. "People are driving by a shooting?"

"No, the shooters are driving by their intended victim."

He still didn't get it. "So… shooters are in the car and they're shooting at another car also driving by? Two cars passing by one another, like that jousting business in medieval times?"

"Not exactly," I said. And so I proceeded to explain to him as well as I could what a drive-by shooting consisted of, exactly. In the meantime, we made to leave the room and look for more possible clues into the murder that had just taken place across the corridor.

"I don't like this," said Brutus.

"What don't you like?" I asked.

"Why, this drive-by shooting, of course. If people are going to start shooting innocent pedestrians, Hampton Cove will turn into some kind of mafia town, with killers on every corner of the street waving machine guns and spraying bullets."

"I don't think we're quite at that stage yet," I said. "And besides, Chase is on top of it."

"Still," said the big black cat. "Drive-by shootings are bad for tourism, Max."

"Bad for your health as well," said Harriet.

But then I guess that was a given, as being shot at is not

conducive to living a long and healthy life. If the bullets don't kill you, the stress just might. We had passed into the room where the murder had taken place, and this time I vowed to go over every possible clue that I could find. The crime scene people had come and gone, and apart from the lone police officer posted at the door, we were the only ones in there. I checked the balcony, and saw that the window was firmly shut from the inside. So if the killer had left that way, he would have had to be Houdini and make a miraculous escape. There was no other exit except the door, where Carlos and Mindy had been, hearing strange gurgles and noises coming from inside the room.

As I thought about this, Norm came buzzing up to me.

"Oh, there you are," he said. "I've been looking for you guys."

"So?" I asked. "Any clues yet?"

"Well, I talked to Bill, who's a good friend of mine. He's a cockroach," he added for good measure. "He says that the prince dropped a piece of buttered toast on the carpet, and also a piece of pork sausage."

"Interesting," I said, though I didn't immediately see the significance. "Did he drop this after he was shot or before?"

"Unfortunately, Bill didn't pay a lot of attention to the prince. He's been having trouble with his wife, you see."

I got a feeling he was eager to get into the trouble in great detail, as it was a topic that obviously interested him, and so I held up my paw. "Just tell me what he did see," I suggested.

Norm seemed disappointed that he wouldn't be allowed to pour the details of his friend's marital life into my ear, but I wasn't in the mood to listen to any more stories about marriage trouble. "No, he didn't see a thing."

"No killer? No intruders?"

"Nothing," said Norm. "But like I said, he wasn't paying attention to what was going on around him. He's in his own cocoon, you see." He sighed. "A little bit like me, in fact."

I glanced around the room, and saw the chalk outline near the door. So was it possible that the prince had let his killer in and had then immediately been shot? What surprised me was that the prince had been alone in his room. No entourage. No bodyguards. No security at all. Not even a servant anywhere in sight. Almost as if he had been traveling incognito.

Heading into the bathroom, I saw that Prince Abdullah had made the effort to hang up his wet towels, something not all hotel guests bother with. It told us something about the kind of man he had been. Neat and tidy and organized. And as I glanced around, I suddenly saw that a message seemed to have been written on the mirror. It was hard to make out, and the only reason I saw it was because I was on the floor and looking up at the mirror from an oblique angle. It wouldn't surprise me if Abe's people had completely missed it.

"What does it say, Max?" asked Dooley.

"I'm not sure," I said, trying to make out what it said. "Looks like… 'You'll pay for this?' Something like that?"

"Pay for what? For his room?"

I smiled. "Hotel management isn't in the habit of writing threatening notes on their guests' mirrors in case they don't pay. No, this must have been left by someone threatening the prince." Though of course it could have been left before the prince had arrived. But since hotel rooms are usually cleaned when a guest leaves, that wasn't very plausible. In which case the prince had been given this warning. A warning he had tried to remove. Unless his killer had done the removing?

It was certainly food for thought, and so I made a mental note to relay this information to Odelia the moment she returned from her visit to this drive-by shooting.

It was shaping up to be a busy day.

CHAPTER 7

When Odelia and Chase arrived at Grover Street, the part of the street where the incident had occurred had been cordoned off and crime scene investigators were checking the bullet holes that had been made in the store facade of Mitzy's Tea Shoppe where the unfortunate victim had been standing at the time of the incident. Though unfortunate perhaps wasn't the right word to describe Mr. Hartshorn, who was one lucky man to have escaped with his life.

"How many?" asked Chase as he walked up to the crime investigator pulling a slug out of the wall.

"I count thirty so far, detective," said the investigator. "Looks like AR-15 ammo."

"Christ. And you're telling me the guy who was shot at wasn't hit? At all?"

"Amazing, isn't it? He sure had Lady Luck on his side. To be shot at with a weapon of this kind and walk away unscathed. It's almost unbelievable when you consider the odds."

"It sure is," Chase grunted as he checked the wall, which

had been thoroughly chewed up. "Where did they take him?" Chase asked a police officer who had been first to arrive at the scene and had managed to preserve the crime scene and prevent it from being contaminated by the onlookers who had arrived in droves.

"Hampton Cove Memorial," said the officer. "He said he was fine, but we thought it was probably a good idea to have him checked out anyway. Sometimes the adrenaline will prevent them from feeling that they've been hit."

"It's almost impossible that he wasn't hit," said Chase. "Especially if they fired straight at him. Where was the van?"

"Right here, detective," said the officer, and showed them how close to the sidewalk the car had been driving. "According to what Mr. Hartshorn told us, the van slowed down as it approached him, the window rolled down and the weapon appeared, then started spitting bullets—that's how he described it: it was spitting at him. Of course, we now know that it was spitting ammo. It was all over very quickly, then the van sped up again and took off."

"License plate?"

"Nothing, detective. Though we are actively looking for witnesses. Mr. Hartshorn himself doesn't remember much. Witnesses we've spoken with say it was an ordinary white van. No decal. One witness filmed the whole thing on his phone but there's no license plate that we can make out, and he didn't get a good look at whoever was inside the vehicle."

Chase rubbed his formidable chin. "Sounds like a professional hit. But why? What does he do for a living, this Rogelio Hartshorn?"

"He's an estate lawyer. Says he was meeting a client, but the client was late, and that's when this van showed up out of nowhere and the gunman started spraying him with bullets."

"Did the client arrive?" asked Odelia.

"Not as far as we know," said the officer.

"We better check to see who this client is," said Chase. He nodded his thanks to the officer. "We'll be out of your hair, Randal. Keep up the good work."

Time to go and pay a visit to Rogelio Hartshorn in the hospital and get his statement.

They drove on in silence, but then Odelia piped up, "You don't think there's a connection with the murder of Prince Abdullah, do you?"

"Too soon to tell, babe, but I don't think so. Seems like two totally unrelated crimes to me."

"Yeah, I guess so. Weird, though, to have two crimes on the same day. What are the odds?"

"What are the odds that this Hartshorn fellow would survive an attempt on his life?"

It certainly sounded like he'd had a miraculous escape, she thought, and hoped the doctors who were examining him wouldn't find that he had been hit after all and that now that the adrenaline had worn off he was suffering some kind of collapse.

In due course, they arrived at the Hampton Cove Memorial Hospital, and after Chase parked in front of the impressive building, they entered and asked at reception where they could find Mr. Hartshorn. The man was still in the emergency ward, and when they arrived there, they found him looking pretty hale and hearty for a man who'd just been shot at. After they had introduced themselves and had produced their badges, he became very talkative.

"I really don't know what happened," he said. He rubbed his nose. "But the doctor says I'm fine. For a moment there I thought he was going to fill me up with water, you know, like they do in the cartoons? And then the water would all start draining out of me through all these bullet holes?" He laughed at his own joke, and even Odelia managed to produce a smile. He looked a little manic, she thought. But that was probably to be expected after what he had been through. "But nothing! Not a single bullet hole to be found. Not a one. Looks like I escaped with all of my vital organs intact, and the rest also. I still don't understand what happened, exactly. Why would these people suddenly start shooting at me, do you know?"

"I'm afraid we haven't been able to get a trace on them yet," said Chase.

"We were hoping that you could give us some more information about what happened," said Odelia. "That would greatly help us find the people that did this to you."

The man scratched his head. He was handsome, Odelia thought, in an understated and bookish sort of way. He was clean-shaven, wore trendy glasses, and kept his hair fashionably long but not too long. He was also wearing a sharp suit that must have cost him a pretty penny.

"So do you have any idea who would want to do this to you, Mr. Hartshorn?" asked Chase.

"Not a clue!" he said, throwing up his hands. "I'm just a small-town lawyer, you know. Estate law. Probably the most boring branch of law possible. All I can think is that it must be a case of mistaken identity. Maybe they thought I was a crime boss or something."

"You were meeting a client?"

"That's right. A potential client. She had sent me a message and asked to meet. She didn't feel comfortable coming down to the office and wanted to meet in town."

"Was it her idea to meet at Mitzy's Tea Shoppe?"

"Yes, she suggested the venue. Though it's a tea shop I've frequented plenty of times, since it's right around the corner from my office, so I thought it was an excellent choice. She asked me to wait for her out front, since she was afraid of walking into the tea shop by herself."

"That didn't strike you as odd?" asked Chase.

The man frowned. "Now that you mention it, it did strike me as a little odd. But then the customer is king, you know." His eyes widened. "Why... do you think this person set me up?"

"It's possible," said Chase. "Do you have her contact information?"

"I have her name and phone number. Marjorie Collett." He took his phone from his jacket pocket and scrolled through his list of messages for a moment, then pulled up the woman's information. "This is her," he said, and Chase dutifully took a picture of the contact details.

"You haven't received any threats lately?" asked Odelia. "Threatening letters, emails, phone calls?"

"Nothing," said the lawyer, shaking his head. "Like I said, I practice the most boring branch of the law."

"And the name Marjorie Collett doesn't ring a bell?"

"Never heard of the woman before," he said.

"No connection to any of your existing clients?"

"No connection at all."

"Any of the cases you're working on right now raise alarm bells?" asked Odelia.

He thought for a moment. "Well, I have been working with a foreign client, which is a little odd, since most of my clients are local."

"Do you have a name for this client?"

"Prince Abdullah. He's a member of the ruling family of the kingdom of Abou-Yamen, a small country in the Middle East. One of the ruling king's sons or grandsons, I believe."

Odelia and Chase shared a look. The man immediately picked up on their sense of surprise.

"What's wrong? Did something happen to the prince?"

"I'm sorry to inform you," said Chase, "that Prince Abdullah was shot dead an hour ago."

CHAPTER 8

Vesta was cleaning a spot on the kitchen window when she became aware of a strange scene playing out in the backyard. It was her son-in-law Tex, and he seemed to be going through some kind of apoplexy. He was shaking his fist at the lawn and shouting at no one in particular, almost as if he was going through some species of mental breakdown. Which didn't surprise her in the least. She had often voiced the opinion to her daughter Marge that Tex worked way too hard. Too many patients and too many long hours spent at the doctor's office he ran in town. If she had said it once she had said it a hundred times that Tex should stop accepting new patients and limit himself to the ones he already had. Most of the doctors they knew had done the same thing since they couldn't keep expanding indefinitely. Or they had joined a clinic where they collaborated with other doctors and shared the workload. But no, Tex had to be the lone hero who kept seeing all the patients and worked all the hours that God sends.

And now finally the man had snapped and had turned into a basket case.

Behind her, Marge entered the kitchen, humming a pleasant tune that was vaguely reminiscent of a hit song on the radio.

"Marge, will you look at this," she said. And when her daughter had joined her at the window, she pointed to Tex, who had resorted to jumping up and down now while still shaking his fist at the lawn. "He's finally gone and lost his marbles, the poor guy."

"What is he doing?" asked Marge, proving once and for all that Vesta knew her son-in-law better than her daughter did. "Why is he wearing his good shoes in the garden? I've told him to wear his old sneakers. Those are his best shoes. The ones he uses when we go out."

Vesta could have told Marge that there wouldn't be a lot of nights out on the town in the couple's near future, but since she didn't want to be the bearer of bad news, she wisely kept her tongue. "It's not the shoes I'm worried about. But the strange behavior. And the cursing, Marge. What's up with the cursing? I mean, what did that poor lawn ever do to him?"

"It's that new bug spray he's been trying out. Clearly, it isn't giving him the results he's been hoping for."

"Bug spray? What bug spray?" The news that her son-in-law was using a new type of bug spray greatly disturbed her, since she considered the backyard her own personal domain and didn't like it when Tex interfered without asking her permission—or at the very least her opinion.

"He picked it up after we saw an ad on TV. It's supposed to be harmless for plants and humans and pets, but lethal to bugs. But I get the impression it doesn't work as advertised."

And since Vesta was not the kind of woman who took this interference into her personal affairs lying down, she immediately yanked open the door and yelled, "What's the meaning of this, Tex! What do you think you're doing spraying YOUR bug spray on MY lawn?!"

"Didn't I tell you about that?" said Tex, but the look on his face told a different story. Clearly, he knew he had broken the unwritten law about who was really in charge of the backyard they shared. "I've been trying to get rid of these chinch bugs. They're destroying the lawn. And I saw this ad last week of a new bug spray that's supposed to be safe and healthy for humans and pets both. So I figured I'd give it a shot." He gestured angrily at a patch of lawn that looked as if locusts had a go at it. The blades of grass were all chewed up. "But look at this. It's almost as if this spray has only managed to make them proliferate even more, instead of killing them. If things go on like this, the whole lawn will be dead within weeks."

It was true they'd been having a lot of trouble fighting this particular strain of very hardy and annoying bugs. The creatures loved the lawn even more than Vesta or Tex did. "Violence is never the answer, Tex," she said. "We have to find some other way to deal with this pest." And since their cats were well-versed in conversing with all manner of bugs and other pests, the only thing she could think of was to ask them to tell these nasty bugs to take a hike. They could move to Blake's Field and feast on grass to their heart's content, and no one would even notice.

"I guess so," said Tex reluctantly. She got the impression he'd been trying his own tough-guy approach on the bugs, since she saw plenty of evidence he'd been stomping around like Godzilla, trying to eradicate the pest. It hadn't helped, as she could have told him.

"I'll talk to Max," she promised.

"Max? What good will that do?"

"Max will talk to the bugs and ask them to vacate the premises," she explained.

"You really think they'll listen to a cat? These are tough bugs, Vesta. Some of the toughest creatures there are. They've survived for millions of years, so they consider themselves to be the top of the heap. They're not going to listen to a cat telling them what to do." He shook his head. "No, we need to show them who's the boss in this here backyard of ours."

Vesta could see that there was no reasoning with the otherwise mild-mannered doctor. Touch his lawn and the man became a killing machine, laying waste to entire swaths of bugs.

And since she didn't feel like getting into an argument with the doctor when he was in this mood, she returned indoors, eager to share her plan with Marge. When she entered the kitchen, though, of her daughter, there was no trace. And since the cats were out as well, she had no recourse but to pick up her phone and call her best friend. Scarlett picked up on the first ring.

"Did you hear what just happened?" asked Scarlett.

"No, what?"

"There's been a drive-by shooting on Grover Street."

"A drive-by shooting? What is this, prohibition redux? Al Capone decided to reincarnate?"

"Luckily, the guy they were aiming for managed to miraculously survive."

"Who is he?"

"Rogelio Hartshorn."

"The estate lawyer?"

"That's right. He handled Dick Bernstein's estate. Did such a great job, too."

"Drugs, probably," said Vesta. "It's always the ones you least expect it from, isn't it?"

"Too bad. I've always liked Rogelio. I've been thinking of

paying him a visit to handle my own estate. Looks like I'll have to find a different lawyer."

"Your estate? What do you want to bother about your estate for?"

"We're not getting any younger, honey. Maybe you should talk to Rogelio, too."

It was a topic she had never given a lot of consideration to, figuring that estate planning was something that the millionaires and billionaires of this world bothered with, not the likes of her. So it surprised her that her friend would have estate planning on her mind, since Scarlett wasn't in either of those two categories. Unless… "You're not secretly a billionairess, are you?"

Scarlett's throaty laugh was all the reassurance she needed. "A billionairess! Me! That's priceless! Oh, Vesta, thanks for the laugh. It's exactly what I needed right now."

"Glad to be of service. Anyway, I've got this idea I need to run by you. Meet at the Star?"

"Absolutely. Can't wait."

And as she disconnected, she wondered if maybe she shouldn't start thinking about her own estate as well—such as it was. She planned to live forever, of course, but still. Unforeseen circumstances and all of that.

CHAPTER 9

Norm wanted to introduce us to his friend Bill, but frankly, I wasn't in the mood to talk to a depressed cockroach. I may be a detective, but that doesn't mean I'm also a psychologist and enjoy listening to stories about marital strife. Besides, not being married myself, I wouldn't know what to advise him. Nor did I have a solution for Norm's issue with having kids.

"But don't you at least have an opinion on the matter, Max?" asked Norm when I told him I couldn't tell him whether to take the leap and have kids or not. "I mean, you're supposed to be the smartest cat in town."

"Being smart doesn't mean that I have to have an opinion on everything," I said. "And so as far as having kids is concerned, I plead the fifth, buddy."

"I have an opinion," said Dooley. "I think you should have kids, Norm. Odelia and Chase had a baby, and even though I was very nervous about the prospect at the time, it turned out very well. Contrary to what I thought, Odelia didn't get rid of us, and nor did Grace turn out to be some kind of monster. She's a lovely little girl and we all adore her. Isn't that so, you guys?"

"We do adore her," said Harriet. "And I like to think that she adores us. Well, I know she adores me, but then I'm extremely adorable, of course, so that was always a given."

"I think she likes all of us," I said. "And equally so."

Parents shouldn't have favorites, but nor should kids. And so I liked to think that Grace loved all of us in equal measure.

"So you think I should have kids?" asked Norm. "What do you think, Brutus?"

Brutus laughed. "You're asking me if you should have kids?" But then his face sagged. "I can't have kids. I've been neutered, you see. So I can't have kids even if I wanted to. And it was done without even consulting me, you know. Nobody ever asked me if I wanted to have kids."

"It's all right, buddy," I said, patting him on the back. I'd forgotten that the topic of offspring was a sensitive one for our friend. And also for Harriet. But mostly Brutus, since he felt he wasn't a real cat ever since he had discovered he'd been neutered. At one time, he even considered getting Neuticles: testicular implants for neutered pets. Lucky for us, he'd dropped the idea, or we'd never hear the end of it, and he'd be strutting his stuff every chance he got.

"I'm so sorry, Brutus," said Norm. "I didn't know."

"How could you?" said Brutus. "Nobody knows. Except my best friends—and of course the people that did this to me," he added bitterly. "Chase's mom and that criminal vet of hers."

"We're all in the same boat here, my friend," I said.

Brutus sighed deeply. "It's a cross we have to bear." He then glanced up at Norm, who had taken up position on top of the big mock-up of a fly, which was a disconcerting sight. "So when you ask me if you should have kids, it's a yes from me. Before these vets get their hands on you as well and excise the miracle of procreation." He gave the fly an earnest look. "Just do it, Norm. Do it while you still can. Before it's too late. Like it's too late for us." He produced a single sob and turned away his face so we wouldn't have to be a witness to his distress.

"You know, I've never looked at it this way," Norm confessed. "But maybe you're right. It's my God-given capacity for procreation that sets me apart from a lot of those less fortunate. So maybe I should put it to good use. And also, that way, the name of Norm will live on."

"So you'll call your kids Norm?" asked Dooley, interested.

"Absolutely. Well, unless they're girls, of course. In which case we'll call them Norma." Our conversation seemed to have perked him up a great deal. "So if you have no further need for me…"

"No, I think for the moment we're fine," I said. "Thanks, buddy."

"You're very welcome, Max. Any time I can be of assistance, just holler."

I had a feeling he was bursting at the seams to procreate, and who was I to stand in the way of nature taking its course?

We watched as he flew off, a song on his lips and a definite breeziness in his wing action, and I think we all thought the same thing: there flew one lucky fly. A fly fly, in other words.

"Okay, so what do we know?" I asked.

"Nothing," Brutus grumbled. "We know nothing!"

"We know that a cockroach is having trouble with his missus," said Dooley. "And also that Norm will be a proud father soon of lots of Norms and Normas."

Brutus gave him a scathing look, and Dooley quickly shut up.

"It's true, though, isn't it, Max?" said Harriet. "So far we don't know a lot about what happened."

"Norm seems to think Carlos and Mindy are the culprits," said Brutus. "So maybe he's right? I mean, they could have done it. Shot the guy and then pretended as if they'd walked in on him lying the floor? It would explain why the killer has vanished without a trace."

"But why, Brutus?" I asked. "Why would people who sell bug spray murder a prince?"

That had him stumped for a moment, but he quickly rallied. "I'll bet he refused to buy their bug spray and so they killed him," he said.

I shook my head. "That makes no sense at all. If every salesperson who met sales resistance in a potential customer would shoot them dead, the world would be full of dead people."

"The world *is* full of dead people," he grumbled. "And people that should be dead, like the vet that did this to me." He was pointing to his nether regions, and I had a feeling that he wouldn't be much help today. And since I felt that our work was done for now, we decided to leave the hotel and go in search of our humans to report. But as we tried to leave the room, we discovered to our dismay that someone had closed the door and had locked us in.

"What's this?" asked Brutus.

"The door is locked," Harriet pointed out.

"It's the killers!" said Brutus. "They know we're on to them and they've decided to make sure we won't spill the beans."

Just like his theory that the bug spray salespeople had killed the prince because he didn't like their product, this didn't make a lot of sense either. But since I could see that I was setting myself up for an argument I couldn't possibly win, I decided to leave well enough alone. And since the window that led onto the balcony was closed, it looked as if we were effectively stuck.

"How did Norm get out?" asked Harriet.

"Maybe he flew through the keyhole?" Dooley suggested.

"Or maybe there's some other way in or out," said Brutus hopefully. As much as he hates not being able to father kids, he hates being locked up even more. Especially as we had no way of knowing when Odelia or Chase might return. Maybe they had no intention of returning at all, but would only notice us missing tonight when they arrived home after a long day at the office. In which case we'd be locked in there for a very long time—with no food or water.

"I don't like this," Brutus grumbled. "I hate being locked up. Being locked up stinks."

I placed a paw around his shoulder. "I'm sorry that you were neutered, buddy, and I'm sorry that you'll never have kids. But can you please lighten up a little? We're stuck in a room with no way out, and it's important that we keep our wits about us, and our mood up."

"Okay, fine," he said without much excitement. "So what do you suggest we do?"

I shrugged. "What can we do? Sit tight and wait until someone opens that door?" Harriet had been humming a little tune, and suddenly I got a bright idea. "You know, maybe you could sing us a song, Harriet," I suggested. "Just to keep the energy up, you know."

"Oh, absolutely!" she said. "What do you want to hear, Max? Any special requests?"

"Just pick your favorite song," I said.

She smiled broadly, happy at the chance of having an audience. Dooley gave me a pained look. "Are you sure, Max?" he whispered. "We *are* in a confined space, you know."

"I know," I said. "But I promise it won't take long before someone opens that door and lets us out."

"I hope so," he said with a sigh. Clearly, he wasn't a big fan of Harriet's talent.

Harriet, undeterred, opened those formidable pipes of hers and burst into song. The sound was enough to rattle the window panes and though I thought I could see the wallpaper coming loose on the walls and falling to the ground, that could have simply been my imagination. Before long, the sound was so devastating that I wished I had brought along a pair of earplugs. But then no earplugs can contend with the sheer power of Harriet's voice. People started pounding the walls of the adjacent rooms, and not even five minutes into her concert suddenly the door swung open and the hotel manager strode in, looking perturbed. When he saw Harriet sitting on top of the bed singing at the top of her lungs, he pressed his hands to his ears, a grimace distorting his features, and approached her the way one approaches a hurricane or twister or some other natural disaster zone. The moment he had reached her, he tentatively removed one hand from his ears, screwed up his face in an expression of sheer agony, and managed to grab Harriet by the neck and pick her up, then drag her bodily from the room.

"Hey, what do you think you're doing!" she yelled.

"This man is saving us, Harriet," I pointed out. I didn't specify who he was saving, but it was enough to make her stop singing, which was a big relief for all of us, and also the hotel manager, who trudged off with Harriet still firmly dangling from his hand.

"We better follow her," said Brutus. "Before we get locked up in here again."

And so we followed the manager as he traversed the hotel with Harriet suspended from his outstretched arm. It was a curious sight, and plenty of guests watched us stride off. When they saw the manager holding Harriet in a firm grip, they broke out into spontaneous applause.

In other words: we had been saved from imprisonment and would soon be reunited with our humans. But instead, the hotel manager took Harriet into his office, and since we were all following him, like those kids chasing after the pied piper, before we knew what was happening, we were locked up again, only this time in the manager's office!

In other words: we'd gone from bad to worse.

CHAPTER 10

Andy Pettey glanced out of the window of his hotel room and shook his head. This town was going to the dogs, and fast. They'd been vacationing in Hampton Cove for close on thirty years now, he and his wife Brandy, but it had never been as bad as it was this year. Caterwauling cats in the next room, people being shot in broad daylight, and now even a murder of an actual prince across the corridor. What was going on? He retracted his head.

"Are they still there?" asked Brandy, who had been glued to the television set in a corner of their room.

"Still there," he confirmed. "Looks like you were right, sweetest. We shouldn't have come this year."

"But where else are we gonna go?" she lamented. "This is our home away from home."

"Well, it's time we found a new home away from home then," he said. "They actually shot a man across the corridor, honey. Shot him stone-cold dead!"

The hullabaloo had been so overwhelmingly loud that they'd both stepped out of their room that morning to see what was going on. Normally not all that interested in meddling in other people's affairs, this time he felt they couldn't stay away, as the noise was preventing them from mapping out their day. And that's when they discovered that their neighbor, an actual prince, had been shot. Shot dead with an actual gun! Right there. In their favorite hotel in what was supposed to be a fairy town. And in the middle of their vacation, no less.

Before long, they'd been interrogated by two police officers, who had peppered them with questions that Andy frankly found extremely insulting. Almost as if they thought *they* were the murderers! Now why would they go about murdering people? He was a retired shoe salesman and Brandy a former nurse. So they were both in the business of saving lives—he through supplying them with the proper footwear, a mission he had always taken very seriously. And she through the loving care she lavished on her patients throughout a long career.

The moment this whole business with the prince was over and done with, they were out of there, Andy thought. And if it was up to him, they'd never come back.

"I don't get it," said Brandy as she half-turned to him. "A drive-by shooting? In the heart of Hampton Cove? But why?"

"I didn't even know they had organized crime here," said Andy, shaking his head.

"They didn't have it last time we were here," said Brandy. "I'm sure of it. Must have traveled over from the big city when things got too hot for them over there."

It certainly seemed as if the ills of the big city were spreading to the country now.

He got up and opened the door a crack.

"What are you doing?" she asked.

"Looking to see if they're gone," he said. As far as he could tell, the room had been sealed off with that yellow crime scene tape the police liked so much, but of the officers themselves there was not a single trace.

"Looks like the coast is clear," he said.

"Good. Then we can finally go down to the beach. Did you order that packed lunch like I told you to?"

"What?"

"Packed lunch, Andy."

"Why are you talking about a packed lunch, woman?" he snapped. "There's been a murder right under our noses, and another one around the corner. We're probably in the middle of a gang war so I think it's time we got out of Dodge. Before these maniacs target us!"

"But why would they target us? We're not rich or anything, like this dead guy was."

Prince Abdullah had been more than merely rich. He had been of noble and royal heritage, according to the one conversation Andy had had with him over breakfast a couple of days ago. He was part of the royal family of Abou-Yamen, he had said, and had plenty of brothers and sisters and nieces and nephews and uncle and aunts, and all of them were princes and princesses, as far as Andy understood. Hundreds of them. But when he asked the prince if he was in town for business or pleasure, the prince had clammed up on him, and had merely smiled and bid him adieu. It was all very mysterious, he thought. And now the guy was dead. So maybe the reason he was in town had something to do with why he had been killed?

"But I don't want to go," said Brandy. "We just got here, and we paid for two whole weeks."

"It's not safe here anymore, honey."

"I don't care! Just look at the streets. They're still teeming with tourists. So why can't we be like them, huh?"

"Because whoever killed the prince must have been

keeping an eye on him. And if they saw that he talked to us, they might come after us as well."

"I don't see why they would," she insisted stubbornly.

"Whatever the reason they killed the prince, maybe they figure he told us about it. And they can't have any witnesses."

"Witnesses to what! We don't know anything!"

"They don't know that we don't know," he said, making her eyes glaze over a little. Even though he loved his wife dearly, he had never been blind to the fact that when God doled out the brain cells, she hadn't been first in line. She hadn't even been part of the first batch.

"Okay, look at it from the perspective of the killer," he said. "He sees us talking to the prince, so he figures we're all part of the same entourage. So who's to say he won't come after us next, huh? And when that happens, I want to be far away from here." And never come back. There were many other places they could visit, up and down the coast. They could head up to Cape Cod maybe, or Nantucket even. And hope this killer didn't follow them up there.

"Let's just head down to the beach," she said. "Forget all about what happened. The police are on top of things and before you know it, they will have nabbed the prince's killer and things will go back to normal."

Clearly, Brandy had no clue. No clue whatsoever. "We're leaving," he said. "Pack your bags." And when she still didn't make any sign of getting a move on, he snapped, "Unless you want to be killed as well?"

She wasn't happy about it, but still did as she was told. And so he started throwing his own stuff into a suitcase as well. The sooner they were out of there the better.

CHAPTER 11

"Prince Abdullah was your client?" asked Chase, much surprised.

The estate lawyer nodded. "No idea why he'd come all the way to Hampton Cove, since I'm sure he must have excellent lawyers in his own country. But it would have been a great coup for me, so I wasn't going to complain." He shrugged. "Though now it looks as if I won't be getting to meet him after all."

"You hadn't met yet?"

"No, we were supposed to meet tonight, over dinner."

"To discuss what?" asked Odelia.

"I'm not entirely sure," said the man. "He hadn't told me what it was he wanted to discuss with me yet. I was hoping he'd send me some more information about his expectations, so I could prepare myself for our dinner, but so far he hadn't."

"So you have no idea why he wanted to meet?" asked Chase.

"He'd written me a letter—an old-fashioned letter, if you please—complimenting me on my work for a friend of his. A man named Isaac Furnish, who works as a tennis coach in one of the resorts along the coast. Apparently Prince Abdullah had been a guest at the resort and had met Isaac. He must have told him about my work, or at least that's what I think happened. How else would he have picked me to do his estate planning for him?"

"So that's what you think he wanted to do? Plan his estate?"

"Can you elaborate, Mr. Hartshorn?" asked Odelia.

"There isn't much to tell," said the lawyer. "Most people don't think about their estate until it's too late—in other words when they're dead. It's important to think about it before you die, so you can plan things in advance, and prevent your heirs from having to pay estate tax."

"Prince Abdullah, did he have heirs, that you know of?"

"No, he wasn't married as far as I know. And he didn't have kids."

"But he was well-off?" asked Odelia.

"Oh, absolutely. One of the richest people in his country. Or at least his family is very rich. He's related to the king, you see. So in that case, it matters who you leave your fortune to, I can tell you that right now. When someone dies intestate, his fortune will go to his next of kin."

"And in the case of Prince Abdullah, this would be…"

"I have no idea!" said the lawyer, spreading his arms. "I'm sure he was going to tell me all about it over dinner. Why? Do you think he was murdered for the inheritance?"

"It's a possibility we have to look into," said Chase. "Though there could be other motives as well, of course."

"And the people who shot me?" asked the lawyer. "What's going to happen now?"

"Now we'll try to find them and put them away," said Chase in that reassuring tone that he did so well.

"But in the meantime? They tried to kill me once, and failed. So you think they'll try again?"

"There's every chance that they will," Chase admitted.

"So..." He gave them a questioning and hopeful look, and Odelia knew what he was going to ask even before he opened his mouth. "Can I have some police protection, please?"

She shared a look with her husband. Uncle Alec wouldn't be happy about this. Police protection meant they'd have to assign an officer, or even more than one, to protect the man until the people who had made that attempt on his life had been caught. It also meant that they couldn't rely on these officers for the investigation, and the station was understaffed as it was.

"I'll ask my uncle," she promised.

"I hope you can give me some protection," said the man. "Otherwise, I don't know what I will do. I mean, I have a business to run, you know, and I can't do it when every time a car passes by the office I have to duck underneath my desk, afraid I'll get shot at again."

"Like I said, I'll talk to my uncle," said Odelia.

And she would, since obviously the man had a point.

They got up and made to leave the hospital room. "Can you... Can you put an officer at the door?" asked the guy. "Or put me up at a safe house or something?"

Odelia smiled. Did he really think the Hampton Cove Police Department would have a safe house at their disposal? "Wait here," she said, and she and Chase left the room to discuss things. Behind them, the lawyer started pacing the floor, nervous and anxious about his safety.

"Are you really going to ask your uncle to assign a babysitter to this guy?" asked Chase the moment they were alone.

"What else can I do? We don't want to see him killed, do we?"

"No, I guess not," said Chase. "But I can tell you right now that the chief doesn't have any men to spare to be some lawyer's babysitter."

"Let's just ask," she suggested. Asking wouldn't hurt anyone, and even if Uncle Alec said no, they might be able to work out some solution on their own.

She put in a call to her uncle and put the man on speaker. But it was as she had expected. The chief had no officers to spare, so no guard duty would be assigned to the estate lawyer. But then he seemed to get a bright idea. "You know, there is one possible solution that I can see."

"And that is?" asked Chase.

"He could stay with you." Chase's jaw dropped, and he opened his mouth to protest. "If you don't mind. It's either that or we'll have to send him home—and risk him being shot."

"But, boss!" said Chase. "We have a family!"

"And so, I'm sure, does this guy. Right?"

"No, he's single," said Chase.

"Even better. Let him stay with you for the time being. Set up the spare room. Just until you catch the people that are behind this business with the drive-by shooting."

"But…"

"The quicker you catch Mr. Hartshorn's killers, the sooner he can go home."

"But chief!"

"That's an order, detective."

Chase's closed his mouth with a click of the teeth. He did not look happy.

"But uncle," said Odelia, "how can we put ourselves in jeopardy for the sake of one man? And we don't even know if he was the intended victim."

"They shot straight at him, honey. Emptied an entire clip at the guy. And you think he wasn't the intended target? Really?"

"Okay, so maybe he *was* the intended target. But putting him up at the house is like putting a bull's-eye on ourselves."

"Nobody will know that he's staying at your place."

"These criminals have ways of finding out, surely."

"Then we'll have to make sure they don't find out." And with these words, he hung up!

God, she thought. Sometimes it sucked to have a police chief for an uncle!

CHAPTER 12

Andy was lugging a suitcase to the elevator, his wife Brandy right behind him, when they came upon a strange scene: a couple were carrying a large mock-up of a fly.

More weirdoes, Andy thought. It certainly strengthened his resolve to kick the dust of this town off his feet. They'd been coming there for a long time—too long, he now realized, and probably should have picked a different place to spend their vacation. The place was going to hell in a handbasket. If it wasn't people being shot, it was nutcases lugging giant-ass flies through the hotel. And as they traversed the hallway, they had to press themselves up against the wall to let the duo pass. As they did, all of a sudden something fell from the fly's innards—if a fly does indeed have innards. As Andy looked a little closer, he saw that it was… a gun!

Christ!

He stared at the gun, and then slowly looked up at the guy carrying the fly. Their eyes met, and in that instant he knew that he was staring into the eyes of a killer.

Crazy, cold, and calculating. Soulless eyes, like black holes! A regular psycho maniac!

In a reflex action, he picked up the gun and pointed it at the guy. Later, when telling the story to his friends back home, and his kids and grandkids at the Thanksgiving dinner table, he would always refer to this moment as his John McClane moment. The one where John decides to take on an entire crew of hardened killers so he can save his wife Molly. He was thinking of Brandy, of course, since either *he* picked up that gun, or the killer did, and got rid of them both by drilling neat little holes into their bodies, the same way he'd done with the prince or king or whatever that Abdullah guy had called himself.

"Stick 'em up, sport!" he yelled at the top of his voice.

"But sir!" said the killer.

"No backtalk from you, is that understood? Put 'em up right now, or I'll put a bullet between your eyeballs. Stick 'em up right now!" he added and gestured with the gun.

The couple slowly put down the mock-up and did as they were told.

And now what? Adrenaline was coursing through his veins, making him a little giddy.

"Brandy, honey, call reception. Tell them we've got the killers of the dead fella right here, and tell them to send up the cops."

"Yes, Andy," said Brandy, sounding a little nervous.

He grinned at the killer. "Thought you could smuggle the weapon out of the hotel in this fly, huh. Well, think again, buddy!"

"But sir," said the killer as he started lowering his hands, no doubt eager to get a hold of his backup gun.

"Keep 'em up!" he yelled.

"But that gun isn't mine!" said the guy desperately.

"Someone must have stuck it inside the mock-up," said the killer's accomplice.

"A likely story!" he said. "Brandy, how's that phone call coming along?" he asked, without taking his eyes off the killer for even a single second. There were lives at stake here —his and Brandy's—and he wasn't taking any chances. Not with these professional killers. Probably hired guns by Abdullah's enemies. Could be the Russians, maybe, or even the Chinese.

"But I promise you that this gun isn't ours!" said the guy. "We've never even seen it before, have we, Mindy?"

"First time I've laid eyes on it," the woman confirmed.

"Keep talking, you gang of psycho killers!" he cried. "Pretty soon you can tell your story to the cops. Let's see if *they* believe you!"

"Oh, God," sighed the guy, looking more nervous now than ever. Andy saw that he was also sweating profusely, which didn't surprise him. Killers had a code. If one of them got caught, instead of spilling the beans to the cops, either they took their own lives, or they were killed by one of their associates. Suicided. He'd seen so many thrillers he knew all about it.

"Yes, reception?" he heard Brandy say. "My husband has caught the killers of that nice gentleman in room 34. Yes, he's holding them at gunpoint. Can you please send someone up to the third floor? Quickly, please. Yes, really quickly. These people look very dangerous." She hung up and said in a breathless voice, "They're sending the hotel detective up to meet us."

"And what about the cops? Where are the cops?"

"The cops, too," said his wife.

"Good," he said, and he waved to the killer. "Up against the wall. Do it! You too, missy. Nice and slow. And don't make me tell you twice, you hear. I've got a really itchy trigger finger."

"But honey, you're not going to shoot these people, are you?" asked Brandy.

"I might," he said, not willing to admit he'd never held a gun in his hands before, and didn't have a clue how to use it. All he knew was that tomorrow morning his name and face would be in their local paper. He'd be the man of the hour. The hero who caught the killer of poor Abdullah! Maybe he'd even get some kind of reward. A medal, handed out to him by the prince's brother or whatever. They might even get a free vacation out of this.

"Oh, honey, you're so brave," Brandy gushed as she clasped her hands together.

"Just doing my civic duty," he grunted as he still kept his eyes locked with the killer's. The man seemed to have developed a sudden weakness around the knee area for he had sagged against the wall and was now sitting on his ass on the floor, giving them a miserable look.

He wasn't fooled by the act. It just meant that the killer's plans had been thwarted. And since he'd done the thwarting, whatever reward was to be given for the killer's capture was all his and his alone! They might even comp them their room. Or give them a nice upgrade!

The elevator door dinged and an entire contingent stepped out. Amongst them, he recognized the hotel manager, but also a burly fella who may or may not have been the hotel security person, and another beefy fella and a gorgeous blonde. The burly fella flashed a badge.

"Chase Kingsley. Hampton Cove police. I'll have that gun now, Mr…"

"Pettey," he said. "Andy Pettey. And this is my wife, Brandy. And those two over there," he said pointing to the killer and his associate, "are the killers of that nice Prince Abdullah!"

All of those newly arrived turned to the couple pressed up against the wall, then at the giant fly on the floor, and marveled at the scene.

"Mr. Perks and Miss Horsefield?" asked the blond babe, sounding surprised.

"It's all a terrible misunderstanding!" the killer cried piteously. "We were moving our mock-up to the car when all of a sudden a gun fell out."

"The killer must have hidden it in there," the killer's associate claimed.

"We didn't do it!" said the killer as he held up his hands. "We had nothing to do with this whole murder business. Like I told you earlier, when the prince was shot, we weren't even in the room with him. We were knocking on his door."

The cop stared at the gun for a moment, which he had placed inside a plastic baggie, and seemed to consider his next course of action. "I would like you all to come down to the station with us," he said finally. "You too, Mr. and Mrs. Pettey."

"But I had nothing to do with this," said Andy. "*I* caught the killer."

"That's for us to decide, Mr. Pettey," said the cop, and Andy didn't much care for the way he said it. And he could already see what was happening here. Probably the killer and the cop were friends—in a small town like Hampton Cove, everyone knew each other. Maybe they were even related. They could be brothers, or cousins! Or best friends since high school!

And now they were going to pin this entire sordid business on him!

Fat chance!

And so he broke into a run. "Brandy, let's go!" he yelled over his shoulder. "Come on!"

"But Andy!" cried his wife. "Where are you going?"

"We're getting out of here before they pin this whole thing on us!" Or worse, murder them so they could get rid of an annoying witness to a crime!

He had gotten as far as the elevator when a powerful hand grabbed him by the neck and dragged him back and down to the carpet. He landed hard, the air being knocked out of his lungs. And as he lay there, he found himself staring up into the cold blue eyes of that burly beefcake of a cop. "Like I said, you're going to join us at the police station, Mr. Pettey. And then you're going to tell us why you suddenly decided to go for a run."

"You won't pin this on me!" he yelled as he tried to fight off this bully. "You won't! I've got friends in high places!"

The cop smiled an icy smile, then dragged him to his feet. "Let's go," he said, and gave him a push in the direction of the elevator. For a moment he thought he might still make it, but then he felt the cold hard steel of a pair of handcuffs being attached to his wrists and knew that he was out of luck.

Looked like they were both done for it. No doubt they'd meet with an 'accident,' their bodies dumped in an elevator shaft, never to be found again. He hung his head. Goodbye cruel world. If only he'd never picked up that gun! He'd wanted to play the hero, and now look where it had gotten him! For a moment he wondered what John McClane would have done, but then he figured John wouldn't have allowed himself to be captured in the first place. As he stepped into the elevator, a pesky fly settled on his forehead for a moment before taking off again.

CHAPTER 13

We had been biding our time in the manager's office when a familiar face came buzzing in through the ventilator grille located above the door. It was Norm, and we greeted him with open arms—so to speak.

"You guys!" he said, sounding a little out of breath. "There's been a development! My suspects have been arrested! So looks like I was right after all!"

"And who are your suspects?" I asked, though I had a pretty good idea.

"Why, the fly killers, of course. I mean, it starts with a single fly, then slowly but gradually they progress to wiping out our entire species, before they finally move on to their own."

"You mean that the bug spray couple have been arrested?" asked Brutus.

"That's exactly right!" said Norm, who looked extremely pleased with himself, I saw. "I knew they were guilty, of course. You develop an intuition for these things. But I'm glad that Chase and Odelia finally saw the light and decided to haul them off to jail."

"How did it happen?" I asked. Knowing Chase, he wouldn't have arrested the couple without probable cause or plenty of evidence to point to them as the culprits.

"The dumbest thing! They forgot to hide the murder weapon where it wouldn't be found. It just happened to fall out of that abomination they think resembles a fly!"

"You mean the gun fell out of that big mock-up?" asked Brutus with a laugh.

"That's right! It fell right at the feet of another guest of the hotel, who immediately had the presence of mind to pick it up and make sure the killers didn't escape. He pinned them down until the cops arrived and hauled them off to the pokey." He sighed happily. "Am I glad this ordeal is over. I mean, it's all well and good to interview a bunch of bugs, but it makes you feel like such a chump, you know? Having to ask a bunch of total strangers a bunch of tough and very personal questions. I don't know how you guys do it."

"It takes practice," said Brutus. "And a certain lack of decorum."

"And curiosity," said Harriet. "You have to be a very curious individual to ask a lot of personal questions. But then I've always been extremely interested in what makes other people—and pets—tick."

"So the killers have been arrested?" asked Dooly. "But that's great! That means our investigation is over!"

"If only we could get out of this office, we might be able to go home," said Brutus as he glanced at the window that was shut, and the door that was also firmly closed.

"Oh, so you guys are locked up in here, are you?" asked Norm.

"Yeah, the hotel manager didn't like it that I gave a free concert for the benefit of his guests," Harriet lamented. "I guess he wants to monopolize all the entertainment, so he can ask for more money. Free entertainment clearly isn't part of his business plan."

"I would open the door for you guys, but I'm afraid I don't have the strength," said the fly. "Though I could always ask a friend—or a couple of friends."

"More flies, you mean?" I asked. "I don't see how that is going to do us any good, Norm."

"Except when they show up in considerable numbers," said Harriet. "Like, a couple of thousand flies? That would get the manager's attention, wouldn't it?"

We all shared a smile, and Norm said, "I'm on it!" And moments later was buzzing through that same ventilator grille again, on his way to carry out another important mission.

"So great that the murder has been solved," said Dooley. "Though I wonder why they did it."

"Probably because the prince proved to be a tough customer," said Brutus. "He didn't want to buy their bug spray so they killed him." He shrugged. "That's what you get when you read all those books on cold calls and the tough approach to sales and taking no for an answer."

"It's probably a new sales technique," Harriet suggested. "When you can't close, you threaten to shoot the customer. And when he still doesn't want to play ball, you kill him."

I didn't think this approach would prove a big hit, but then I'm not a salesperson, of course, and I've never taken a sales course. Maybe it was de rigueur right now to use tough measures when trying to make a sale. Though I still found it a little odd that this couple, of all people, would have killed the prince. Especially since they claimed to have been standing outside the door when the guy was being shot. Unless they had lied about that, of course. Killers often show a certain reluctance to tell the truth. I guess it comes with the territory.

"How long do you think we'll have to wait here, Max?" asked Dooley. The four of us had jumped up onto the manager's desk to have a better overview, and we sat on top of a stack of documents—possibly contracts that needed to be signed, and bills that needed to be paid. Some of them bore the monikers 'past due,' 'overdue' or even 'final notice.'

"Well, Norm will have to amass his troops, so that can take a while," I said. "And also, he has to guide them to this office, which will also take a little time."

"It won't be long," said Harriet confidently. "There are flies everywhere, and they'll be only too happy to assist a fellow fly in his attempt to spring us from jail."

A sort of buzzing sound now reached my ears, and I got the impression that Norm was on his way. Very soon an entire horde of flies were pouring through that grille above the door, and the room was starting to fill up with the winged creatures. There were hundreds of them—possibly thousands, and as the four of us hunkered down on the desk to await further proceedings, Norm positioned himself in front of us, a triumphant expression on his tiny face. "Well, what did I tell you? I was going to get you out of here, and I've kept my promise!"

"Are these all friends of yours, Norm?" asked Harriet, a sort of awe in her voice.

"Friends? No, this is my family!"

"But... there must be thousands of them."

Norm shrugged. "I have a fairly small family, but I still love them, you know. Hey, you gotta work with what you've got, right?"

We all marveled at the sheer volume of flies filling up the room, and when Norm told us this was just his closest relatives, with the rest of his family all lingering outside the door, I didn't want to be in the manager's shoes right now, with his hotel nicely filling up with flies.

I just hoped he'd get the message and open that darn door!

CHAPTER 14

Vesta and Scarlett had managed to get their usual seat on the Star Hotel's alfresco dining area, and had ordered their usual drinks: a cappuccino for Scarlett and a hot chocolate with plenty of foam and chocolate sprinkles for Vesta. And she was just about to reveal her grand scheme to get rid of those annoying bugs that were eating the lawn when a fly landed on her spoon. She waved it away with an annoyed gesture.

"Isn't it a little too early in the season to have flies harassing us?" she asked as she watched the annoying insect with a baleful eye.

"It's never too early in the season for flies, Vesta," said Scarlett as she took a dainty sip from her cappuccino. "So what's all this about a new bug spray that Tex is trying out?"

"Well, it doesn't work, that's the long and the short of it." She saw that another fly had descended from the rafters and had taken up position on the table and was eyeing her hot cocoa with a longing eye—or a thousand longing eyes, since flies have those weird facet eyes that make them see a lot of stuff at the same time. A pretty cool feature. Even though she wasn't a big fan of flies—who is?—she had to admit she had a certain admiration for the creatures.

"Okay, so the bug spray doesn't work?" Scarlett prompted when she faltered once again.

"Hm? Oh, yeah, it doesn't. And now our plants are all being devoured by these weird-looking beetles. And so I was thinking that I could ask the cats to open negotiations with the bugs. Maybe convince them to pass along to greener pastures, you know."

"Can they do that?"

"Oh, absolutely. I mean, there's nothing those cats of mine can't do. They're very clever and extremely resourceful."

"You're so lucky that you can talk to your cats," said Scarlett, not for the first time. "I wish I could talk to Clarice. She's such a sweetheart, and I've grown so fond of her, so if only we could chat, that would be amazing. She could tell me all about her hopes and dreams."

"I still contend that you could learn their language," said Vesta. "It's probably just a knack you can pick up. Like driving a bicycle or parallel parking."

"I can't parallel park for the life of me," said Scarlett. "And as far as riding a bike goes, I haven't done that in years."

"But surely you could learn to talk to your cat, couldn't you? Look, all you have to do is listen very carefully when they're trying to tell you something. Really focus, you know."

"I've tried," said Scarlett. "Lord knows I've tried. But it's all just gibberish to me, honey."

"Okay, I'm going to talk in cat language now. Listen very carefully, all right?" and she proceeded to tell her friend that her hot cocoa was very delicious.

Scarlett laughed. "That sounded so funny!"

"Well, it wasn't funny," said Vesta. "Let's try again. Listen carefully to what I'm saying. And try to listen with your heart, not your mind, if that makes sense."

Scarlett made a face. "I don't even know what that means."

"It means that you can't look at this rationally. It's a knack, something you need to work on—one moment you don't understand a single thing, and the next you've got it. Okay? Here we go." This time she told her friend that there were too many flies around for the time of year and she was going to make a complaint to the hotel manager if he didn't get a handle on things and remedy the situation. She eyed her friend expectantly. "So what did I say?"

"Um... that you're hungry and you want a cookie?"

"No!" she sighed. "You're not trying hard enough, honey. Do you even *want* to do this?"

"Of course I want to do this!" she said. "But it's difficult, you know."

"It's not difficult. It's easy. Okay, one more time. Listen carefully."

"I am listening carefully with my ears and my heart and whatever else."

"Okay, here goes." But before she could launch into another sentence spoken in the language of cats, a dozen flies all attacked her cup of hot chocolate at once, and as she watched in dismay, she saw that several of them managed to end up floating on top of her chocolate! "Oh, my God!" she said. "Did you see that? A mass suicide attempt!"

"Death by drowning in chocolate milk," said Scarlett as she made a face. "Fish them out, the poor creatures."

"I will not fish them out!" said Vesta. "They did this to themselves!"

"Fish them out I'm telling you!" And when Vesta didn't make a move, she proceeded to use her little spoon to fish out the flies and save their lives. "Always be kind to animals," she explained.

"Flies are not animals," said Vesta. "They're bugs, and not

the best bugs either. They spread all kinds of diseases, didn't you know? One minute ago they're traipsing around Farmer Giles's cows, feasting on their poop and urine, and the next they're all over my hot chocolate! It's disgusting, that's what it is." She pushed her cup away. "I'm not drinking this—no way."

"Okay, so you were saying?" said Scarlett as she leaned in. "Something about flies, right?"

She gave her friend a look. "I didn't even speak feline this time. Just plain English."

"Oh, so that's why I understood. I thought I'd finally gotten the knack, as you say."

Vesta sighed, and decided that maybe there was no use to this thing. Maybe it was, as her granddaughter always claimed, a genetic thing that couldn't be taught. If they could teach it, by now Tex should have gotten it, or Chase, or even Alec. But no—only the women in her family could understand their feline darlings, with men being excluded from taking part in the great feast of reason and the flow of soul as they conversed up a storm with their cats.

More flies now descended on the scene, and as she gaped at them, she saw that there were hundreds of them—maybe even thousands! Or millions!

"What is going on!" she cried as she got up. Flies were all over the place: on her clothes, on her head, in her hair, on her purse!

"It's an invasion!" said Scarlett, pushing her chair back. Other customers also got to their feet, all expressing their dismay at this sudden takeover by the collection of flies.

Several waiters came hurrying out of the bar and used their towels to get rid of the flies, but the creatures simply flew up and then settled down again.

"Let's go," she said. "Before we get eaten alive—or covered in fly crap."

"We haven't paid," Scarlett reminded her.

"And we're not going to!" said Vesta. "If they can't even protect us from these horrible beasts, they don't deserve to get paid."

She walked off the terrace and saw to her surprise that Chase and Odelia were escorting a bunch of people to squad cars. All four of them had their wrists cuffed behind their backs and looked deeply unhappy.

"What's going on?" she asked.

"Can't talk now, Gran," said Odelia.

"But… that's Tex's bug spray guy!" she said, pointing to one of the people under arrest. She recognized his picture from the YouTube video she had watched. Also, the fact that one of the police officers was carrying a giant mock-up of a fly was a dead giveaway. "Good for you," she told her granddaughter. "People like that should be arrested. Selling bug spray that doesn't work—it's a crime!" She now understood why there were so many flies in the hotel. The manager had probably used the bug spray these people were selling and more flies had come—just like Tex with his chinch bugs.

Which gave her another one of her bright ideas—she was on fire today!

"Hey, were they guests of the hotel, by any chance?"

"I'm sorry, but I can't stay and chat, Gran. I have to get these people to the station." And with these words, her granddaughter was off after her husband and the line of arrestees.

"Let's go," she told Scarlett.

"Where are we going?" asked her friend.

"To get us a couple of cans of bug spray," she said, and set foot for the entrance to the hotel. "I've just had a great idea."

"Uh-oh," said Scarlett. "I mean," she quickly amended when Vesta shot her a dirty look, "that's great news!"

CHAPTER 15

Garland McNerlin didn't know where he had to pay attention first. Guests were complaining, his staff needed him, and those horrible flies were everywhere! Pooping on the walls, pooping on the dining room tables, pooping on the gleaming surfaces in the kitchen—not so gleaming now after hordes of those bugs had passed through. All in all, it was as if he was living through his own personal disaster movie, and he didn't have The Rock to save him! If the Star survived this ordeal, he'd send a prayer to Saint Julian, patron saint of hotel keepers!

"They're everywhere, sir!" said Christel, his receptionist, a young woman who hadn't been in the job for more than six months but was still doing an admirable job under difficult circumstances. First a murder, now this. When would this horrible day end?

"We have to do something," he said as he watched the buzzing of the insects with a panicky eye. His guests were either calling the front desk or complaining to him in person, and he couldn't be seen doing nothing!

"But who do we call?" asked Christel.

"The exterminator, who else?" But then he remembered that those bug people had dropped by the hotel a couple of days ago and he had signed a contract for a substantial quantity of their bug spray. The problem was that it hadn't arrived yet. Maybe they had brought a couple of cans with them for their demonstration today? He remembered the police had put them up in one of the rooms after the murder of that prince, and they had even put their giant fly in there for the time being. So maybe they had also stored their product in the room? He certainly hoped so!

And so he hurried off in the direction of the elevator, hoping to find that little stash and empty a couple of cans of the stuff into the lobby to get rid of the pesky pest.

The elevator took forever to arrive, so he decided to take the stairs. Halfway to the third floor he regretted this rash decision, as his heart was pumping like mad and his legs were trembling from the exertion. He still arrived there in one piece and made a beeline for the room where the police had put the bug people before they had been carted off in the paddy wagon. He held his key card against the sensor and the door clicked open. Much to his surprise, he found himself face to face with two elderly ladies he recognized as regular clients of the hotel. Reading from left to right, they were Vesta Muffin and Scarlett Canyon!

"What are you doing here?" he asked.

"We could ask you the same thing," said Vesta in that belligerent fashion that was a hallmark of the lady's irascible personality.

"I'm the manager," he reminded her, puffing out his chest a little.

"And I'm a guest of the bug people," said Vesta.

He piped down immediately. "You wouldn't happen to know if they brought along some samples of their bug spray, would you? We've got a fly emergency on our hands."

"I know all about that. Those flies are everywhere. And you should be ashamed of yourself, Garland," she added as she poked his chest with one of those bony fingers of hers.

"It's not my fault!" he cried, the injustice of this remark stinging him like an adder.

"It's your hotel, so you must have done something to attract those flies," she said, and there was a certain logic in what she was saying, he couldn't deny.

"Look, where is that bug spray?" he asked, feeling that it wasn't in his best interest, or that of the hotel, to waste a lot of time standing there and arguing.

"They've been arrested, you know."

"Who's been arrested?"

"Why, the bug spray couple, of course."

"Do you know if they left their samples behind or not?"

"It doesn't work, you know."

"Doesn't work? What do you mean?"

"My son-in-law tried it on some bugs that have been using our backyard as their personal restaurant, and instead of getting rid of them, more are arriving. Our backyard is full of them."

"Nonsense," he said. "It's bug spray. It kills bugs. It says so on the label." And since he refused to listen to this annoying old woman even one second longer, he started looking for the cans of bug spray surely these salespeople must have brought along with them. He finally found a suitcase full of them and smiled. "Found them!" he cried.

"Give me a couple of those," said Vesta.

"Why? I thought you said they didn't work?"

"Oh, but they do work, only not as advertised."

He reluctantly handed over a couple of the cans, and then took the entire suitcase along with him. He'd pay the couple later. If they really had been arrested, they probably wouldn't mind if he used their stash to rid the hotel of a clear and present danger.

He dragged the suitcase out of the room and then down the elevator this time, to arrive in the lobby. He then proceeded to hand the members of his staff who were on hand to try and get rid of those flies several cans of the stuff, and instructed them to apply them liberally.

"But sir," said the head of his housekeeping department. "Isn't this bad for our guests?"

"Absolutely not," he said, remembering the sales pitch Carlos Perks had given him. "It's only lethal for the bugs, but perfectly safe for humans and pets both. So spray these to your heart's content, and let's get rid of those damn flies!"

And to set the right example, he directed a nice cloud of bug repellent at a flock of flies that had chosen the reception desk as their landing strip. They immediately dispersed, and his heart made a little jump for joy in his chest. Victory!

The moment he had distributed all the cans among his staff, he hurried to his office, hoping to put in a phone call to the exterminator. Mostly the guy assisted them when they had mice or rats in the kitchen, or cockroaches or lice or bedbugs in the rooms, but this time he'd have to handle a more mundane pest: a fly invasion!

The moment he swung wide the door of his office, a swarm of the creatures attacked him, and he reeled back in horror. The beasts were everywhere: on his face, in his hair, even in his nostrils, his ears, his mouth! He fell to the floor, and tried to get them off him—to no avail!

"Aaaaah!" he cried in dismay. "Aaaaaaaah!"

And as he lay there, a victim of this attack, he was vaguely aware of four cats traipsing all over him and then taking off. They were the cats he had captured and locked up in his office. More pests! But at least they weren't as obnoxious or pestilential as those flies.

Oddly enough, the moment those cats had left his office, the flies all took off, and before long his office was free of them. But as he glanced around, he saw they had pooped on every available surface—even his laptop and the pictures of his wife and kids he had on his desk.

He sank down onto his chair and buried his face in his hands. What a day. What a day!

CHAPTER 16

We escaped the hotel through the lobby, which was teeming with Norm's family members. For some odd reason, several hotel staff members were emptying cans of bug spray throughout the lobby, saturating the atmosphere with the concoction and creating an unpleasant and frankly toxic air quality. It didn't stop the flies from buzzing around the lobby, though. On the contrary, instead of dropping dead like… flies, they seemed to love the stuff, and more and more of them were flocking to have a whiff of the aerosol.

"Odd," said Harriet. "The more they spread this bug spray, the more bugs arrive."

"We shouldn't call them bugs, though, should we?" said Dooley. "They are Norm's family, so we should treat them with the respect we owe him—especially since he saved our lives."

"How do you figure that?" asked Harriet.

"Well, that manager is clearly colluding with the bug spray people, who are rabid killers, so he could have murdered us, and cut us up into little pieces and fed us to the dogs."

"Do dogs eat cats, though?" asked Brutus. "I doubt it."

Dooley had to think about that one. "No, I guess you're right," he said finally. "Dogs would never eat cats. We might not always get along, but they wouldn't want to be any part of that."

We had arrived on the street and I was glad to breathe some fresh air again—insofar as the air on Main Street can be called fresh, of course, as there were still plenty of cars zooming past, making our crossing of the street a hazardous venture. But we made it across in one piece, and decided to recover from our harrowing adventure by paying a visit to our friend Kingman.

"Hey, you guys!" he said, and gestured to two bowls of kibble placed at his feet. "Take your pick. One is a new brand called Brand A and the other is a new brand called Brand B. Not the real names, of course. Pick what you like best and I'll inform Wilbur accordingly."

I stared at the two bowls, and couldn't see a single difference between the two types of kibble. I then took a sniff and they smelled exactly the same. Finally, I took a nibble and had to admit that I didn't taste any difference either. I turned to our friend. "Are you sure these are two different brands? I mean, they are exactly alike in every respect as far as I can tell."

My friends had all taken the sniffing test, the tasting test, and the visual test also, and were busy devouring some of the kibble so they could make up their minds.

"Just tell me what you like best, Max," said Kingman.

"It's a trick question, right?" I said. "Brand A is exactly the same as Brand B."

"No, it's not," Kingman insisted. "They're different brands, and your mission, should you choose to accept it, is to decide which one is the better choice: A or B. And please don't tell me you can't choose. It's a task Wilbur has given me, and I want to give him my full report."

In this case, Kingman's full report consisted of him eating the remainder of the most popular kibble, so Wilbur knew which one he had to order from his supplier. It was a simple method, not unlike the screen tests Hollywood studios like to organize for their movies: testing different endings or cuts of their films so the audience can choose which one they like best.

"I think I like Brand A the most," said Dooley. "It's got more flavor."

"But they're exactly the same!" I cried. "They both have the same flavor!"

"I don't think so," said Dooley. "I think Brand A has more flavor than Brand B."

"How about you, Harriet?" asked Kingman. "What do you think?"

"I like Brand B the best," said Harriet, smacking her lips.

"I prefer Brand A," said Brutus, putting his vote in the hat.

They all turned to me. "Looks like you've got the deciding vote, buddy," said Kingman. "'Cause I also vote for Brand B. So that's two against two, with your vote breaking the tie."

"But I like them both!" I said, not comfortable being put in this position.

"Well, you can't choose both. You have to choose one. So which one is it going to be?"

I glanced from Dooley to Harriet to Brutus and back to Kingman. "I don't know," I confessed. "They both taste exactly the same to me, they look the same, and they smell the same. In other words: they *are* the same!"

"They are not," Kingman insisted. "I saw the bags myself. They were different brands!"

I was shaking my head and wondering how to respond. I

didn't want to deceive anyone by choosing the wrong brand, but finally, I had it. "So how about you ask a couple more cats? Then maybe you'll have a large enough sampling to really make an informed choice."

"Excellent idea, Max," said Kingman, pointing his paw at me. "And that's exactly what I've been doing all morning. I've asked every single cat that's passed by to have a taste, and you know what they said?"

"That they're both the same kibble?" I asked.

"No! That they're both equally bad, so Wilbur shouldn't order either." He sighed. "Which is a message he won't like to hear."

Just then, Gran and Scarlett came ambling up. They both looked pleased as punch for some reason. Which never bodes well, as Gran can sometimes be accused of having a mischievous mind. "What's going on here?" she asked as she saw us gathered around two bowls of kibble.

"Kingman wants us to choose between these two different brands of kibble," I explained. "Only I don't taste any difference. They're exactly the same to me."

"Let me have a taste," she said, and stooped over and picked up a piece of kibble and put it in her mouth. We all watched on, consternation written all over our features.

"But Gran, you can't eat that!" I cried.

"And why not?" she asked. "It's made from meat, isn't it? With some extra ingredients thrown in to provide a balanced diet for you guys. So why shouldn't I eat it?"

"But… it's made for cats!" Dooley cried.

"Oh, well, since I'm basically an honorary cat, you won't mind, will you?" And with these words, she picked up a piece of kibble from the second bowl and put that into her mouth as well. She made a face. "Tasty, but with a slight tang that I don't know if I like."

"Did you just eat the cats' kibble?" asked Scarlett, looking the same way we did: full of surprise at Gran's initiative.

"Okay, I think I've got it," said Gran. "I'll pick the first one. It's got the exact same taste as the other one but I like the label more." She pointed to the two bags positioned on a rack next to us. One was green with black and the other red with brown undertones. "I like the colors on that one," she said, "and that's why I'm gonna pick it. Hey," she added when we gave her a look of exasperation. "Packaging is everything —we all know that to be true. Can I help it that the folks who created Brand B don't know the first thing about designing the right packaging for their product, no matter how tasty or nutritious it's proven to be—and how healthy for the creatures?" She then directed a curious look at Wilbur. "What's gotten into your human?"

"Oh, don't mind him," said Kingman. "He's been counting every single item that leaves the store, and then checking his inventory every hour, on the hour. Someone's been stealing from the store, you see, and Wilbur doesn't like it."

"Who would?" said Gran. "Anyway, I like Brand A the best. So how about you guys?"

"I like Brand A the best also," said Dooley, happy as a clam that he had picked a winner—or at least Gran's winner.

"Good for you," said Gran, well pleased, as she gave him a pat on the head. "Okay, so there's something I need to run by you guys. Would now be a good time?"

I glanced around, and since nobody seemed to be paying us any mind, I nodded. "I guess so."

"Okay, so Scarlett and I have all this bug spray, see—the bug spray that has the opposite effect from what it's supposed to do?"

"You stole it from the salespeople's room?" I asked.

She gave me a scathing look. "Of course we didn't *steal* it! We *borrowed* it. And since they're both in jail right now, they're not going to miss a couple of cans of the stuff, will they?"

I had no arguments, so I simply shrugged.

"Okay, so here's what we're going to do," said Gran. "We're going to feed it to the dogs, and then when the mutts proliferate, we'll know that our experiment was a great success."

"What do you mean?" I asked. "What experiment? What mutts?"

"Or maybe we should feed it to the mice," said Gran, not paying any mind to my question. She turned to her friend. "What do you think, feed it to the dogs, or to the mice?"

"Or rats," said Scarlett. "If I were you, I'd find a couple of nice big rats and use it on them."

"Maybe we will do that," said Gran. "We'll feed it to the rats and when they proliferate—and they will, since this spray has been put together entirely the wrong way, apparently—we'll know we've got a goldmine on our hands. A goldmine!"

We all stared at her. "What are you talking about, Gran?" asked Dooley, always nervous that his human has finally gone cuckoo and will have to be put into an institution for the insane.

"Don't you see?"

"Um... no?" said Dooley.

"What is one of the biggest crises that has hit this nation and a lot of other nations also?"

"Um…. unemployment?" Harriet suggested.

"Inflation?" Brutus said.

"Hypertension?" I ventured.

"Wrong!" she cried jubilantly. "All wrong! The biggest crisis that has struck this great nation of ours is the dwindling birth rate!"

I honestly didn't see what the dwindling birth rate had to

do with bugs, but I had a feeling we would get to it—eventually.

"Okay, so women and men are less fertile, all right? It's a real thing. I saw a documentary about it on the Discovery Channel. Remember, Dooley? You even told me that humans should be more like cats, since cats don't have this issue."

"Oh, right," said Dooley, his face clearing. "Humans really *should* be more like cats. Or flies. Norm told us that a single fly can have upwards of hundreds of kids—did you know?"

"No, I didn't know that," said Gran. "But it doesn't surprise me. Okay, but let's forget about flies for a moment, and focus on humans. So women can't have babies, and have to go through round after round of IVF, right?" She held up a can of bug spray and shook it for good measure. "This is going to put a stop to all of that. We'll simply hit them with the spray. Zap! And pop!"

"Zap and pop?" I asked.

"We zap them and out pops a baby! Crisis averted!"

Somehow I didn't think it would be as easy as that, but since I hate to rain on Gran's parade when she looks so happy, I merely smiled and said, "I like your thinking, Gran. Very creative!"

"I love it," said Dooley. "Zap and pop! Problem solved!"

Gran grinned and actually rubbed her hands the way supervillains do in the movies. "Oh, you guys. We're going to be so rich! We might even get the Nobel Prize for medicine!"

"It's not medicine," I reminded her. "It's a bug spray."

"Who cares," she said, shutting me down without delay. She held up the bug spray. "This is going to be the biggest revolution for women since the invention of the pill!"

"Zap and pop," said Dooley. "Genius, Gran! Absolute genius!"

CHAPTER 17

We returned home feeling a little dizzy after the kind of day we'd had.

"So… Gran is going to spray women so they can have more babies?" asked Dooley.

"Something like that," I admitted, though the plan seemed a little extreme, even for Gran.

"Don't you need FDA approval before you can bring a drug to market?" asked Brutus.

"Pretty sure you do," said Harriet. "Otherwise, anyone can sell any drug and claim any benefits. Heck, I could bring a drug to market that promises to give cats gorgeous fur like mine, even though I fully well know it's simple genetics." She preened a little.

We had settled on the couch, and I had every intention of taking a long nap before I ventured out again—if I ventured out at all. I might stay on that couch for the next twenty-four hours to catch up on my sleep.

"Norm did a great job, didn't he?" said Dooley, proud of our little winged friend. "He caught the killers, and he also managed to free us from that horrible hotel manager."

"He did a wonderful job," I admitted as I yawned widely. Though I still had my doubts about whether the bug spray people were responsible for the murder of Prince Abdullah. After all, I still couldn't see a possible motive. Why murder their client when they were about to pitch their new and improved product to him? It didn't seem logical. Then again, humans aren't exactly the most logical species, and oftentimes they don't need a reason to do anything.

I had just closed my eyes when Odelia entered the room via the front door. Chase was also with her, and they seemed happy to see us.

"You guys!" said Odelia. "For a moment, I thought you were still at the hotel."

"Oh, Odelia, did we have an adventure!" said Dooley as he practically jumped up into her arms. She hugged him close, and he proceeded to fill her in on the details of what we had been through and the ordeal we had suffered at the hands of that evil hotel manager.

"And so the flies saved you?" she asked finally.

"The flies did what?" asked Chase as he opened the fridge looking for something to eat.

"The flies saved the cats from being locked up by Garland McNerlin," said Odelia. "He thought they were making too much noise after guests had complained."

"Is that a fact?" said the cop, not seeming all that interested in our ordeal. Then again, he probably had more important things to deal with than a couple of cats being locked up. An actual murder and also a drive-by shooting.

"Did you find out who tried to shoot that poor man?" asked Harriet, who must have been reminded of the same thing.

"Not yet," said Odelia as she put Dooley back down. "So far, we don't have a single lead."

"We do have some CCTV footage," said Chase. "And a

video a bystander shot on his phone. But that hasn't given us much to go on."

"Fake license plates," said Odelia clarified. "And a stolen vehicle."

"So we still have no idea who was gunning for the guy."

"He sure was lucky, though," said Brutus. "Imagine being shot at and surviving the ordeal."

"Thirty bullets fired," said Odelia, "and not a single hit. He's thanking his lucky stars."

"I sure do," said a man as he walked into our living room.

We all stared at him, and I asked the obvious question first: "Who is this guy?"

"Oh, that's right," said Odelia. "I almost forgot. This is Rogelio Hartshorn. He will stay with us for the time being. Or at least until we've managed to identify the people behind the attack."

"And I wanted to thank you again," said the man, who was tall, dark, and handsome, I have to say. He was also dressed to impress, in a fancy, and no doubt expensive, suit. "This can't be easy for you. And if you prefer I stay at the hotel..."

"Nonsense," said Chase. "You wouldn't be safe at the hotel —or anywhere else for that matter. No, you're staying with us and that's all there is to it."

"I'll show you to your room," said Odelia, and led the man up the stairs. I saw he was carrying a single suitcase, so at least that told us that he wouldn't be staying long.

Dooley asked the next obvious question: "Does he have pets?"

"I don't see any pets," said Brutus. "I mean, if he did have any, he would have brought them, right?"

We all turned to Chase. But of course the cop couldn't enlighten us. He's one of those rare humans who can't talk to cats. He was grinning, though, so I had the impression he knew exactly what we were thinking. He can't talk to us, but he can read us very well after having spent so much time with us, and has an unfailing intuition about what keeps us up at night.

"Okay, so you don't have to worry about a thing," he assured us. "Rogelio is only going to be here for a short time. Like I said, until we manage to find out who's gunning for him."

"So... we're a safe house now?" asked Brutus. "Is that it?"

"And we're his bodyguards," said Harriet sadly. "Which means we'll have to protect him with our lives, you guys. Like the Secret Service. Catch a bullet for him if we have to."

We all gulped in dismay. "But I don't want to protect a total stranger with my life," said Dooley. "I haven't even been trained as a bodyguard so I wouldn't know what to do."

"Dooley is right," said Brutus. "We didn't receive any training. So maybe Chase should send us to a training course so we know what to do if those maniacs return and start shooting up the place?"

"Nobody will shoot up the place," I said. "They don't know that Rogelio is here, so they won't come looking for him."

"These people have ways," said Brutus. "They always find their man. And when they do..." He gulped, and made a slicing motion across his throat.

Dooley's lip quivered. "But I don't want my throat cut, Brutus!"

"Nobody wants their throat cut. But that's not going to stop these people from trying."

"Nobody's throat is going to be cut," I said. "Chase knows what he's doing, and so does Odelia. Otherwise, they wouldn't have agreed to Rogelio staying with us." After all, they not only had themselves to think of but also the four of us—and Grace, of course.

Just then, Marge came walking in through the sliding

glass door, carrying the little girl on her arm. When she saw how perturbed we all looked, she gave us a look of concern. "What's wrong?"

"There's a man staying here who's wanted by some very bad people," said Dooley tearfully. "And when they find out that he's here, they're going to shoot him, like they did earlier, and we have to catch a lot of bullets for him and then they're going to slice all of our throats!"

Marge turned to Chase, who was checking something on his phone. "Is this true?" she asked.

The cop turned to her. "Hm?"

"The cats are saying that a man is staying here who was shot at, and the men who did it will come looking for him."

"They won't," said Chase. "Since they have no way of knowing he's staying with us. So we're all perfectly safe. As long as nobody blabs about Rogelio."

"Is that his name?" asked Marge.

Chase nodded. "Rogelio Hartshorn. He's upstairs with Odelia. She's showing him his room." He took Grace from Marge's arms. "And how was your day, princess?" he asked as he lifted the girl up into the air. She squealed with delight.

"I had a great day!" she said. "I got to hold a frog. He was cold and slimy, and I loved it!"

"You got to hold a real frog in your hands?" asked Brutus.

"I did! He was hopping around in the backyard of the daycare center, and Chantal said only one of us could hold him, and only for a few moments, so we wouldn't scare him. And she picked me, and I got to hold him!" She held out her hands, which looked a little grimy. "See? I haven't washed my hands yet!"

She then rubbed her hands in her daddy's hair, and we all winced. Chase didn't mind, though. Also, he didn't know that now he would be smelling of frog until he took a shower.

Odelia returned with Rogelio in tow and introduced the

man to her mom. She also impressed upon the librarian that she couldn't breathe a word to anyone about the presence of the lawyer in our home.

"I'm so sorry to hear they shot at you," said Marge. "Any idea who is responsible?"

"No idea," said the man. "Though I have a lot of important clients, so any one of them could be behind it, though I fail to see the reason why." He directed a look at Chase, who must have suggested this theory.

"Like I said, inheritances are tricky business," said the cop. "When there's a lot of money involved, or even a little bit of money, people do strange things. And since you seem to be in the middle of things, I suggest the reason for the attack can be found in an inheritance matter."

"I'll go through my files again," said the man. "But I really can't think of anyone who would want to do this to me."

"You're a notary?" asked Marge.

"An estate lawyer. I handle the legal matters when people want to handle their estates and their legacies. But like I said, I can't think of anyone who would want to kill me over it."

"So no contentious cases?" asked Odelia.

The man shook his head. "Nothing out of the ordinary."

Gran now entered the house, and when she saw the handsome lawyer, did a double take. "It's Rogelio Hartshorn, isn't it?" she said, holding out her hand. "Vesta Muffin. You handled the estate of one of my best friends. Dick Bernstein?"

"Of course," said the lawyer. "I remember Dick."

"We haven't met, but I live next door and I'm in the business of making couples happy."

The lawyer smiled. "Is that a fact?"

"Absolutely. I guess you could call me an inventor, an entrepreneur, and also a fairy godmother all rolled into one."

"Rogelio will be staying with us for the time being," said

Odelia. And she proceeded to tell her grandmother the same thing she had told her mom.

Gran made a show of zipping her lips. "My lips are sealed," she promised. "Your secret is safe with me, esquire."

"Oh, no formalities, please," said the man. "I don't stand on protocol, and certainly not in the current circumstances when you're pretty much saving my life."

"You will dine with us tonight, of course?" said Marge. "My husband would be very happy to meet. He's been dying to get our estate handled, but we never seem to get around to it."

Odelia stared at her mom, and so did Gran. "You want to arrange your estate?"

"Of course," said Marge. "Doesn't everyone? I mean, not that there's a lot to arrange. We're not exactly billionaires," she said with an apologetic smile to the lawyer. "But still, it would be nice to know that if something were ever to happen to me or Tex, that everything has been taken care of."

"If you'd like, I can ask my PA to make an appointment," said the lawyer, but then seemed to remember his current circumstances. "I'm not going to my office, though, am I?"

Chase shook his head. "No office for the time being, I'm afraid. Until these men are caught, you're not going anywhere, Mr. Hartshorn."

"Oh, shoot. And I've got a stack of files on my desk, calls to make, clients to see…"

"Don't you have a partner who can take over from you for the time being?" asked Odelia.

"I do have a partner, but he's on vacation right now. In the Bahamas. But then he cheered up. "I'll work from home. I've done it before."

"I'm afraid I can't let you do that either," said Chase. "Doing so might reveal your current location, and we can't have that."

His face sagged. "But… can I talk to my clients over the phone at least?"

"I think it's best if you don't," said Chase.

"I won't give them my current location," said the man. "Or even tell them what's going on."

"It'll be all over the papers tomorrow," said Odelia. "So they're bound to ask a lot of questions. Questions you won't be able to answer. So it may be best to sit this one out, sir."

"Rogelio, please," he said with a look of concern. "Okay, so maybe I'll send a message to my personal assistant. Tell her to cancel all of my appointments. And I'll send a message to my associate. Maybe he can cut his vacation short."

"That would be a great idea," said Chase. "You can always make up for it later, when things have settled down again, and the people who are after you are behind bars."

"And how long will that take?" asked the lawyer.

"I'm afraid I have no idea," said Chase, giving it to him straight, as was his habit.

"Of course," said the lawyer, nodding. "I understand. Well, do what you can, detective, and in the meantime I'll just have to keep my head down and stay out of trouble." He produced a nervous laugh. "Because next time these people shoot at me, I might not be so lucky."

CHAPTER 18

"Max?"

"Mh?"

"This man, this lawyer. Why is he really staying with us?"

"Because people shot at him, remember? And he didn't like being shot at, so now he's making sure they can't find him and try again."

"But why did they shoot at him, Max? Isn't he a good lawyer?"

I laughed. "I'm sure he's a fine lawyer."

"If he's a bad lawyer, maybe his clients got so upset with him that they're trying to murder him," Dooley explained, and I had to admit there was a certain logic in that.

"It's possible," I said, since we hadn't ascertained yet why these people had shot at the guy.

"It could be a case of mistaken identity," said Brutus. "They could have the wrong man entirely, and the real target is still out there, and in danger right now."

"The truth of the matter is that we don't know," said Harriet. "And maybe we'll never know, since these killers are obviously highly trained professionals, and they're not going to allow themselves to be caught that easily."

"If they were highly trained professionals they wouldn't have missed," said Brutus.

"Or maybe they missed on purpose," said Harriet. "Have you thought about that?"

None of us had thought about that, because it didn't make any sense.

The four of us were seated outside, on the deck, in a bid to get away from the busy and quite feverish atmosphere that seemed to have descended over our otherwise cozy little home. Tex and Marge had decided to consult the lawyer on their estate planning, and also Gran and Scarlett, and even Odelia and Chase were starting to see the benefits of having things set in stone in case something happened to them. The only ones who weren't interested in any estate planning were the four of us. But then I guess we don't have a lot to leave to any beneficiaries. Cats aren't caught in the rat race of materialism and capitalism in the sense that we aren't into collecting token items of material wealth on a continuous basis. No expensive Teslas for us, or the latest iPhone. No large mansions or expensive clothes or fashion accessories. Though it is true that from time to time Harriet will get bowled over for some tiara she can put in her hair.

"I think he probably made a mistake," said Dooley, still trying to elaborate on his theory. "He made a mistake with one of his clients and now they're out to get him."

"What kind of mistake?" asked Brutus. "He's an estate lawyer. What mistake could he possibly make that would have a client put out a contract on the man?"

Dooley had to think about this one, but before long he had his answer ready. "He probably gave someone's fortune to the wrong person. Instead of giving it to Barbara with a B he gave it to Margaret with an M. And now Barbara is mad at him for losing out on a large fortune, and she's paid these contract killers to get rid of the man."

We all smiled at this. It seemed a little farfetched, and something that was more at home in the febrile mind of a screenwriter at the Lifetime channel. But since I didn't want to discount any theory at this juncture, I merely nodded and closed my eyes. I was still hopeful that I would get some solid nap time in, even though our couch had been taken over by our family waiting in line for an opportunity to consult with the estate lawyer. He had promised that the least he could do was give Odelia's family access to his services for free, and that hadn't fallen on deaf ears. Even Uncle Alec and Charlene had shown up and were waiting their turn to find out about their options. All in all, it looked as if Rogelio would have his work cut out for him!

"Okay, I think it's time we headed off to cat choir," said Harriet as she got up and stretched. "Are you guys coming?"

"I'm not sure I want to go," I said. "I really could use a nice long nap."

Harriet gestured to the house. "No way you're getting any nap time in tonight, Max. Better to join us for cat choir and then when we get back, hopefully, this bunch will have gone to bed."

I glanced in through the window and saw that the lawyer was seated at the dining room table, discussing ways and means of structuring their estate with Odelia and Chase, while Uncle Alec, Charlene, Marge, Tex, Gran, and Scarlett awaited their turn on the couch. Looked like it was going to be a long evening for the lawyer, who was having to work harder than ever.

"Okay, maybe I'll join you," I said.

Harriet was right. I wasn't going to get any nap time. Unless I headed over to Tex and Marge and found a place to sleep there. But as it happens, I like to take my naps in my favorite spots, and those are all located in Odelia's little home, which is also my own home. Dooley likes to move between the two homes, and Harriet and Brutus consider the Poole home theirs.

We headed out and took the little path that separates both houses to arrive on the sidewalk. And we had just emerged out front when I saw that a white van was parked at the curb that I had never seen there before.

"Odd," I said. "I wonder whose van that is."

My friends all studied the vehicle. "Maybe Marcie and Ted got a new set of wheels?" Brutus suggested.

"Or Kurt and Gilda?" said Harriet, referring to our other neighbors.

Unfortunately for us, it was one of those vans with tinted windows, so we couldn't see who was inside. I thought this was all very suspicious, especially coming on the heels of the assassination attempt on our friendly lawyer guest, and so I figured that maybe it was a good idea to talk to Chase and have him check this van out.

We all returned to where we had come from to alert the cop. We ventured into the house through the pet flap, forming a conga line of four, and trudged up to Odelia. "There's a van parked out in front that looks suspicious," I told her.

"Better go and take a look," Brutus suggested.

"It could be the killers," Harriet added.

Odelia gave her husband a quick glance, but he was so busy listening to the lawyer that she couldn't very well tell him that her cats had just seen a suspicious van parked across the street from the house. The lawyer might think his hosts were two nutcases.

"I'll go and take a look if you like," said Grace.

"Nooo!" we all yelled as one cat.

"You better stay here, honey," said Harriet. "It's too dangerous out there for you right now."

"Suit yourself," said the little girl. "But I think I have a right to be involved if a bunch of strange men are watching the house. I mean, it's my house too, you know. My mommy and daddy have even told that lawyer the same thing."

I smiled and gave her a slight stroke of my tail. "I know you have every right to know if someone is watching the house," I said. "But these men could be after our guest. And if that's the case, they might have guns and might shoot first and ask questions later."

"Okay, fine," she said, but didn't look happy to be excluded. "But I'll have you know that I'm a big girl now. And that I can take real good care of myself. Even Chantal said so today. She said, 'Grace Kingsley, you are a real busybody!' And that's a big compliment."

I could have told her that busybody isn't really much of a compliment, but since I didn't want to burst her bubble, I didn't. Instead, I toddled over to Marge and told her the same thing I had told Odelia. She proceeded to whisper the message into her brother's ear.

Uncle Alec had been watching a news bulletin about Abou-Yamen. About a famine that had ravaged the country a couple of months ago, and how the United Nations had to step in. He reluctantly dragged his attention away from the television screen, and took out his phone. Moments later, he had asked for a patrol car to check the suspicious van parked out in front.

"So easy when you're the chief of police, isn't it?" said Brutus. "All you have to do is pick up your phone and bark an order, and people jump to attention and do what you tell them."

And since cats are essentially extremely curious creatures,

we all hurried out of the house again to see what would go down once the police arrived. We weren't disappointed: the moment a police car appeared at the top of the street, the van's driver immediately started up the engine and was off at a rapid clip, peeling away from the curb like hell for leather, tires screaming. Clearly, these people had nefarious designs in mind. It told us that somehow our guest's new location must have already been revealed, and he wasn't safe anymore.

The police officers must have come to the same conclusion, for they parked in front of the house, got out, and walked up to the front door. Moments later, they stood conferring with Uncle Alec, who didn't look happy about this state of affairs. As we watched, the lawyer was escorted from the premises, bundled into the police car, and they took off with him.

Looked like our guest was no longer our guest.

"Where are they taking him?" asked Dooley.

"To a safe place," said Brutus as we watched the taillights of the police vehicle fade away in the distance.

"But... isn't our home safe?"

"Not anymore," said Brutus. He looked grim. "Someone must have blabbed."

Uncle Alec thought the same thing, for he stood at the door opening with Chase, and the two cops looked extremely unhappy.

"There's a mole at the police station," said Brutus.

Dooley seemed surprised by this. "I didn't know moles lived in police stations. Don't they prefer to live underground?"

"It's not that kind of mole, Dooley," I said. "It's the human kind. The kind that spills secrets to criminals in exchange for money."

"In other words," said Brutus, "the weaselly kind of mole."

This had Dooley stumped completely. "But... an animal

can't be a mole and a weasel both, Brutus. They're different creatures altogether."

"Not in this case they're not," said the police cat. "But Chase is going to nail this nasty piece of work. Just look at his face."

We all looked at the cop, and it was clear that he was going to root out this mole if it was the last thing he did. For putting our guest in danger, but more importantly, for putting Chase's family in jeopardy as well. Things just got real!

CHAPTER 19

We were just about to take off in the direction of town to join cat choir when Gran and Scarlett came out of the house and expressed the same intention. "Ride with us," said Gran. "And we'll drop you off at the park."

And since I've never been the most sporty cat, this sounded like a great idea. And so the four of us took up positions on the backseat of Gran's little red Peugeot, and soon we were off.

"There's one thing I want to do first, though," said Gran as she clutched the steering wheel tightly. "I want to pay a visit to the couple that is locked up in my son's jail."

"Are you sure you want to do this, Vesta?" asked Scarlett. "I mean, we could wait until they're released. I'm sure they're innocent, and Alec will understand this was all just a concatenation of circumstances."

Dooley laughed at this. "A concatenation of circumstances! Those aren't even real words!"

But Gran didn't seem to think it was all that funny, for she frowned. "Knowing my son, he'll never let go of that couple. He'll hold on to them until he's forced to let them go. He's stubborn like that. Like a dog with a bone. And also, they're the only suspects he's got."

"Why do you need to talk to these suspects?" I asked.

"We need to get our hands on more of that bug spray if we want our new business venture to succeed," Gran explained. "We need gallons and gallons of the stuff, so we can start selling it to women looking to have kids."

"But… don't you think this is all a little unethical?" I said. To be honest, I wasn't feeling all that sanguine about Gran's plan. To give hope to women who couldn't have kids seemed cruel somehow, and downright illegal. Especially since this stuff hadn't been tested on humans.

"It's perfectly ethical," Gran assured me. "In fact, we're giving these women exactly what they want: a baby! What could be more ethical than that?"

"But it's bug spray, Gran," said Harriet. "Surely you can't use bug spray on humans?"

"And who says I can't? It's just like that slimming drug, what's its name?"

"Ozempic?" Scarlett suggested.

"Exactly! Did you know it's not a slimming drug at all? It's diabetes medicine! The fact that people lose weight is an unexpected side effect. And the same is true about this bug spray."

I didn't think the Ozempic people would appreciate their drug being compared to bug spray, but then Gran was on a roll, and I had a feeling we wouldn't be able to move her from her point of view, not even with a crane or a bulldozer. And so I figured we might as well go along for the ride. And maybe she was right. Maybe this bug spray did have as its unintentional side effect that it stimulated procreation in mammals, as she seemed to believe. Though a mammal is still an entirely different beast than a bug, of course.

"Maybe I'll get pregnant," said Harriet. "Wouldn't you like to have babies, snowflake?"

Brutus gave me a look of panic. Even though he sincerely regretted having been neutered, the prospect of being a dad took him by surprise. "Um, absolutely. I would *love* to have babies."

"Then let's have some." She tapped Gran on the shoulder. The old lady jumped up and jerked the wheel to one side, causing the car to swerve and almost swipe a pedestrian off the sidewalk. "Honey, don't distract me when I'm driving!" she cried. "What is it?"

"Can you zap me with your bug spray? Zap and pop? I want to have babies, also."

Gran gave her a smile. "Absolutely. In fact, if you like, I'll test the spray on you before I start using it on women." She gave me a look in the rear-view mirror. "Just to humor Max. I don't think it's necessary to test the stuff, since my gut tells me it will work exactly as I anticipate."

I didn't like the fact that she was going to use Harriet as a test subject—a guinea pig, so to speak—any more than I liked that she would use it on women, but I could tell that she wasn't going to budge, and so I wisely kept my tongue.

We had arrived at the police station, and we all got out. Entering the station, Gran and Scarlett walked up to the desk sergeant, a new hire I'd never seen before. Probably fresh out of police academy. Her name was Maria and she seemed a little nervous. She was sitting ramrod straight behind her desk, a pair of oversized earphones on her head, and talking into the mic. "Yes, sir, I'll send a patrol car immediately." She disconnected. "A man complains that his neighbors are organizing a party and he can't sleep. Is it always so busy at night here?"

"Oh, absolutely," said Gran. "Especially in the summer, with all the tourists descending on the Hamptons en masse."

She tapped the desk. "I want to pay a quick visit to a couple of prisoners. Carlos Perks and Mindy Horsefield. How do I go about that?"

"But... are you their lawyer, Mrs...?"

"Muffin. Vesta Muffin. I'm not a lawyer but I *am* your boss's mother. And this is my friend Scarlett. I'm the president of the neighborhood watch, and Scarlett is my second-in-command. It's important that we talk to these people about some neighborhood watch business."

The girl looked like a deer in the headlights. This was a contingency she hadn't been trained for. But then she got an idea. "I'll call the chief, shall I? He's in the building right now. Some kind of emergency, apparently." And before Gran could stop her, she was already calling her boss's phone. "Oh, hi, Chief Lip," she said. "It's Maria. The new desk sergeant? I have a woman here who claims to be your mother. She wants to see a couple of prisoners. Something about a, um, neighborhood watch?" She listened for a moment, then nodded. "Yes, sir. I'll tell her, sir. Thank you, sir. Good evening, sir." She disconnected and gave Gran a wide-eyed look. "I'm afraid your son doesn't want to see you right now. He told me to tell you to go home."

"Oh, the gall of that man!" Gran cried as she shook her fist. "To think I've raised such a disrespectful boy!" She tapped the desk. "Tell him I'm not going anywhere, and if he doesn't let me see the prisoners, I'll file a complaint with the police oversight commission!"

"Do we even have a police oversight commission?" asked Scarlett.

"If we don't, we should start one immediately. My son needs oversight—lots of oversight!"

"I—I'll tell him right now," said Maria nervously. She pressed a button on her phone and moments later was in communication with the chief once again. "Chief Lip, your mother tells me she's going to file a complaint with the police oversight commission if she can't have access to the prisoners right now." She grimaced when his response came back, and even had to take off her earphones. We could hear the chief yelling through the device. Maria gave us a sheepish look. "He doesn't sound very happy, Mrs. Muffin. He says not to bother him again or else."

"I'll give him something else," said Gran, rolling up her sleeves. And then she was taking off in the direction of the station proper, Scarlett on her tail, the four of us picking up the rear.

"Shall I tell him you're coming?" Maria yelled, but Gran didn't even deign to respond.

"What is a police oversight commission, Max?" asked Dooley.

"I'm not sure," I confessed. "But probably it has something to do with keeping an eye on the police. Making sure they do what they're supposed to do."

"I'll bet Gran would love to be on that commission," he said. "She's always finding things that can be improved upon. She's very creative that way."

"I hope this won't take long," said Harriet. "I really need to be at cat choir. Shanille told me last night she wants to introduce a new song into the repertoire, and I don't want to miss it."

"What song would that be?" asked Brutus.

"I'm not sure, but I think she said it was a power ballad? I do love a good power ballad."

We had arrived at the main room where all the police officers have their desks, but it was empty, and the lights were off, so it looked as if the force had retired for the night. Moving on, we heard voices further down the hall, and when Gran slammed into her son's office, we discovered that he and Chase were in a meeting. They both looked up when we arrived.

"Didn't I tell you to go home?" asked the chief unhappily.

"You don't get to order me about, sonny boy," said Gran, planting her fists on her hips. "Now what's all this about me not being allowed to see the prisoners? I'll have you know that I have very important matters to discuss with them. Matters that are a matter of life and death."

"Go away," said Uncle Alec as he waved a tired hand.

Gran bridled. "I will not go away!"

"Don't you have a neighborhood watch patrol to go to or something?" the chief asked.

"I have a business meeting with my business associates to attend, and I intend to attend it right now!"

"Oh, for crying out loud," said the chief, getting up from behind his desk. "Chase, can you please escort my mother and her friend from the premises? Thanks."

And for the first time in her life, Gran was being escorted out of the police station instead of into it. It certainly was a novel experience, and judging from the way she yelled up a storm, she didn't like it very much!

Scarlett went quietly, as is her habit, and the four of us followed along.

"All this walking around has made me very hungry," Brutus lamented.

But if we thought we were off the hook, it turned out that Gran had other plans. "Follow me!" she said the moment Chase had escorted us out of the building and told us to go home and have a good night's sleep and come back in the morning. "I know how we can have our meeting!"

And she started sneaking off in the direction of the jail cells, which are located at the back of the building. It wasn't long before we arrived there, and Gran stood on her tippy toes and approached a barred window. "Psssst!" she loud-whispered. "Psssst! You guys in there!"

A face appeared, and I saw that it belonged to the man who had been lugging that giant fly around that morning.

"What do you want?" asked the man.

"You the bug spray fella?"

The guy paused for a moment. "Yes, I am he."

"I have a business proposition for you," said Gran. She gestured to Scarlett. "My name is Vesta Muffin, and this is my business partner Scarlett Canyon. Together, we want to buy some of that bug spray from you. Gallons and gallons of the stuff. The more you got the better!"

The guy seemed both surprised but also pleased. "That can be arranged," he said. "In fact, I have a nice big stock ready for shipment in our warehouse right now. We were supposed to ship it out to Abou-Yamen as soon as the contracts with Prince Abdullah were signed, but unfortunately, he died this morning."

Gran waved an impatient hand. "I know all about that. His loss is our gain. So how much?"

"How much what?"

"How much of the stuff can you ship to us immediately?"

"We have ten thousand drums ready for shipment," said the guy. "Each drum holds fifty-five gallons, so that's half a million gallons, give or take. They're loaded onto pallets already."

"That's great. I'll take all of them," said Gran.

"So are you in the agricultural business?"

"No, I'm in the fertility business," said Gran, causing the guy to give her a strange look.

"Okay, so as soon as we're out of here, I'll draw up the contracts and we're in business."

"That sounds great," said Gran. "And when do you think you'll be out of here?"

"There's a gross miscarriage of justice being perpetrated," said the man. "Someone planted the gun that was used to murder Prince Abdullah in our mock-up fly, and so the police think that we're involved somehow. But we're not."

A second face now appeared. It belonged to the man's fiancée, and she seemed curious to see who these clients could be, that were so eager to negotiate a deal they couldn't wait until they'd been released. "Hi," she said. "I'm Mindy, and I'm the vice president of Zap, Inc."

"Shouldn't that be Zap & Pop, Inc?" asked Dooley.

"Shush, Dooley," said Brutus. "Let the grown-ups talk."

"Pleased to meet you," said Gran, and held up her hand. It was a little awkward to shake hands through the barred window, but somehow they managed, and moments later a deal was made for ten thousand drums of bug spray to be delivered to Gran's home as soon as the contracts were signed and the money was transferred. If this was a strange way of doing business, none of the business meeting attendants seemed to mind.

Suddenly, from an adjacent window, two more faces appeared. They belonged to an elderly couple, and they didn't look happy. "What's with all the racket?" the man grumbled. "Can't a person sleep peacefully?"

"Keep out of this, buddy," said Gran. "This is a private meeting, and you're not invited."

"You're accomplices of the killers, aren't you?" said the guy in response. "I'll tell the guard that you're out here, schmoozing with the killers, and they'll arrest you and throw away the key—just you wait and see!" He retracted his head, and we could hear him yell, "Guard! There's more killers! Better arrest them before they get away!"

"I think we better get out of here," Scarlett suggested.

"Yes, better go," said Carlos Perks. "The police in this place are really dumb, especially the chief of police, who must be just about the dumbest chief of police I've ever met in my life."

Gran had to laugh at this. "Oh, buddy," she said. "You've just made my day! The dumbest chief of police! I love it!"

And with these words, she said goodbye to the couple for now, and we were off. We had just started in the direction of the front of the building when all of a sudden a loud voice behind us exclaimed, "Rogelio Hartshorn! Show your face, Rogelio Hartshorn!" Much to our surprise, a familiar face appeared in a third window. It was the lawyer, and he seemed curious to know who was calling his name. "I'm Rogelio Hartshorn," he said. "Who are you?"

In response, an automatic gun started spitting out bullets and hammering the wall with hot lead. Rogelio's head retracted just in time—or so I hoped—and the rest of us all dove for cover!

CHAPTER 20

"I didn't even know he was in there!" Brutus cried as we all hid from the volley of bullets aimed at the police station.

"They must have figured it was the only way to keep him safe!" I yelled back over the noise of gunfire.

"Max, I'm scared!" said Dooley.

"No need to be scared," I assured him. "They're not gunning for us but for the lawyer."

"This is not good for my voice!" said Harriet as she clutched her mate's paw. "It's a well-known fact that stress is bad for the vocal cords. If they keep this up, I'll have to press charges."

"Join the line," I said.

In the distance, police sirens could be heard, and I had a feeling it wouldn't be long before the area was swarming with cops. These gangsters had quite the nerve to attack an actual police station! And since I'm a curious kitty, I decided to take a closer look at the criminals responsible for the attack. I snuck from behind the bush we were using for cover and over in the direction of the gunfire. As I approached I saw a white van parked in the field behind the police station, and in front of it, two men were positioned, both wielding automatic weapons and using the police station for target practice. And as I glanced up at them, I saw that they looked very familiar to me. They were none other than Jerry Vale and Johnny Carew!

My friends had followed me and seemed as surprised as I was to see these two.

"But... That's Jerry and Johnny!" said Brutus. "What are they doing here?"

"Playing gangster," I said. "Isn't it obvious?"

"But it's not really their shtick, is it?"

"Looks like they've changed careers again," said Harriet.

"I don't like this, Max," said Dooley. "Guns are dangerous."

"You can say that again," I said. The brickwork of the police station certainly had never been designed to take so much violence and destruction being wrought upon it, and we saw how pieces of brick dropped to the ground, and entire chunks of wall tumbled down.

"Do you think we've got him, Jer?" asked Johnny as he paused the hail of bullets.

"Not sure," said his partner in crime.

"Think we should go and take a look-see?"

But the sound of sirens was approaching fast now, and so the two crooks thought better of it. "I'm sure we got him," said Jerry. "And if we didn't, we'll get him next time. Let's go!"

The two gangsters jumped into the van, and moments later they were off at a fast clip. But since I didn't think it was a good idea to let them get away like this, I decided in a sort of split-second decision to follow them. And since the back of the van was open, I jumped in.

"Max, where are you going?" my friends asked. I saw they

were chasing after me, so I urged them to keep up. It wasn't long before the three of them all jumped in after me. The van bucked and bumped on the uneven terrain, and the door was slammed shut.

"Are you sure this is a good idea?" asked Harriet.

"Not really," I said.

"Johnny and Jerry like us," said Dooley. "Even if they find us, they won't hurt us, will they?"

It was a question I didn't know the answer to. But I sincerely hoped he was right. After the van reached the road, Jerry sped up, and we were propelled back against the van door by the sheer force of the acceleration. It looked as if we'd have to sit tight and hope for the best!

"I hope that the lawyer is all right," said Dooley. "He still has to make sure that all of our humans' estates are in order before they die." Then he seemed to realize what he was saying and put a paw to his mouth. "Oh no! They're all going to die, aren't they? That's why they're making their wills and arranging their estates!"

"Nobody is going to die, Dooley," I said. "Least of all our humans, who are all young and in the prime of their lives."

Brutus grinned at me. "Always the optimist, aren't you, Maxie baby?"

"I try to be," I said virtuously.

His smile vanished. "Let's hope this trip from hell won't prove to be our finest but also our final hour."

The van was slowing down, and moments later there was some bumping and shaking again as it hit a dirt road. After a while, the van brusquely pulled to a stop, and we heard doors slam.

"Looks like we've arrived," said Harriet. She coughed. "Oh, Shanille isn't going to like this. I was supposed to sing one of her power ballads tonight, and instead I'm ruining my voice because of all this stress. It's not good, you guys—and I blame you, Max!"

She gave me a look that wasn't all that pleasant to be on the receiving end of, and I shrugged. "I'm sorry. It was a spur-of-the-moment sort of thing."

"You did good," said Brutus. "We can't let them get away with this. I mean, Hampton Cove is a pleasant town, and we can't have Johnny and Jerry shooting things up for no good reason."

"I'll bet they have a very good reason," I said. "Money."

"You think someone is paying them to shoot at the lawyer?" asked Brutus.

"Absolutely. Everything Johnny and Jerry do, they do for money, so this time won't be any different."

We tentatively approached the cabin of the vehicle and peered out through the windshield. We saw the two crooks heading towards what looked like an old farm, and the sight of it gave me some bad memories from the time they had abducted all the cats of Hampton Cove and locked us up in one of these places. I saw that the window on the passenger side was open, so I climbed up and then took the jump down to the ground below. My three friends all followed suit, and moments later, we were stalking in the direction of the farmhouse.

Light was on inside, and we jumped up onto a windowsill to look in. I saw it was the kitchen, with Johnny seated at the table and Jerry busy putting something into the microwave.

"Looks like they're holed up here for now," I said. And since we knew enough, I decided that it was time to head back into town, to alert the cavalry so they could raid the place and put these two under arrest.

And we would have made it out if not Dooley had accidentally hit an old tin pot located on the windowsill. It fell to the ground with a loud clanging sound. Immediately, an irate-looking Jerry appeared, and when he saw the four of us staring back at him, a wide but cruel smile spread across his face. "Well, if it ain't the kitty cats! Fancy meeting you here!"

Before I could react, he had grabbed me by the scruff of the neck and had supplied the same service to Dooley. Behind him, Johnny was there to collar Brutus and Harriet, and as I released a sigh, I knew that this was going to be a long night.

CHAPTER 21

Odelia was beside herself when she heard what had happened. The police station shot to pieces? Her cats missing? How could this happen? And how had the culprits found out that Rogelio had been locked up at the station—the same mole again? It was imperative that Chase get to the bottom of this mess, and also her uncle.

All of the police officers had descended on the station, and when she arrived, she was met by Chase and her uncle, who had been inspecting the damage. The exterior wall of the cell block had been shot to pieces, but the structure was intact. Plenty of stucco was on the ground, and bullet holes attested to the carnage that had been brought to bear on the old station house.

"None of the prisoners have been hurt," said Odelia's uncle. "And that's the main thing. The rest we'll fix with some plaster and cement—no problem."

"But how did they know that Rogelio was in there?" asked Odelia.

Her uncle shrugged. "Someone must have told them—

there's no other explanation possible. Someone on the inside."

"Just like before," said Chase. The detective was grim-faced. He didn't like the prospect that one of their own was in league with the gangsters.

"Organized crime seems to have come to Hampton Cove," said Uncle Alec sadly. "And I'll be happy to see them leave again."

"Have you discovered why they're targeting Rogelio specifically?" asked Odelia.

Her uncle shook his head. "Nope. No idea. And he doesn't seem to know himself."

"The only thing I can see that is of some significance," said Chase, "is that one of his clients was Prince Abdullah."

"Do you think there's a link between the two cases?"

"It's possible," said her uncle. "But if there is, we haven't found it yet. Have we, Chase?"

"Nothing yet," said Chase. "But it's the only thing that makes sense. A murder and a shooting—two shootings... there simply has to be a connection that we're not seeing yet."

They glanced up at the prison block and saw that Rogelio stood looking down at them, following the conversation intently. "Maybe you should take me someplace a little safer?" he suggested. "I mean, I hate to be a nuisance, but I'm not liking this being-shot-at routine."

"This is the safest place for you right now," said the chief a little curtly. He seemed to personally blame the man for the state his police station was in, and maybe he was right.

Was Rogelio holding out on them? It didn't seem to be the case, but then you never knew, of course. He was, after all, a lawyer, and as everyone knows, part of a lawyer's job description is to lie convincingly and flawlessly. Or at least that was the impression she sometimes got.

"So what about my cats?" she asked.

Her grandmother and Scarlett had been talking amongst themselves and now joined the conversation. "I saw them run off after the van," said Gran.

"And I saw them get into the van," said Scarlett.

"And that's the last we saw of them."

"All of them? All of them got into that van?" asked Odelia, aghast.

Gran and Scarlett both nodded. "I'm afraid so."

"They're so brave," said Scarlett. "So very brave."

"Did you recognize the shooters?" asked Chase.

"No, I'm afraid we never got a good look at them," said Gran. "But maybe the cats did. They were much closer. Scarlett and I spent most of the time hugging the dirt, didn't we?"

"Let's hope they're fine," said Odelia, though frankly she wasn't very happy right now. Neither with her grandmother, who had brought the cats along on this crazy adventure, and had tried to gain access to the prisoners even though Uncle Alec had strictly forbidden her to. And also with Rogelio, for bringing this terrible violence into their lives.

She knew it was unreasonable of her to blame the man, but she couldn't help it.

"We have to find them," she told her husband. "If we find the cats, we find the shooters, and we can put this whole thing to bed. And hopefully discover the link between the shootings and the murder of Prince Abdullah."

"On that note," said Chase, "I've discovered something interesting. Remember Wilbur filed a report of someone stealing stuff from his store? I checked the CCTV footage today, and guess who the thief was?"

Since she had absolutely no idea, she shrugged.

"Prince Abdullah!"

"But... why would a prince steal things from a general store?" asked Uncle Alec. "That makes no sense whatsoever."

"Maybe he didn't know he had to pay for the items he took from the store?" Chase suggested. "If he's a member of his country's ruling class, maybe he's not used to shopping for himself and so he simply takes things and expects someone else to foot the bill?"

"It's possible," said Odelia. She could imagine that being as rich as the prince was, he probably never did his own shopping or washing and cleaning or any of those daily chores. And so when he found himself in a strange town, he might have decided that Wilbur would simply send the bill to the palace, or wherever he was living in Abou-Yamen.

"Anyway, another problem solved," said Uncle Alec as he dragged a weary hand through his meager mane. "So how are we going to find the cats? Any suggestions?" He gave Odelia a weak smile. "We've been here before, haven't we?"

Her uncle was right. The cats had been kidnapped before, and they had found them that time, so there was no reason they wouldn't find them now. Still, she wouldn't feel easy in her mind until they had located them and they were home safe and sound.

"We could use the same method we used last time," she suggested.

"Which is?"

"Ask our neighbors' dogs to find them for us."

Chase puffed up his cheeks and blew out a breath. "Do you really want to wake up the Trappers in the middle of the night?"

"Yeah, can't we simply find a police dog who can offer us the same service?" asked her uncle.

"If you can find us a police dog in the middle of the night," said Odelia, "we won't have to bother the Trappers." The good thing about the Trappers was that their sheepdog Rufus was familiar with the cats, and there was no doubt in her mind that he would be able to find them.

"Okay, you win," said her uncle. "Let's go and wake up the Trappers. But if they complain, you handle it, deal?"

"Deal," she said, and turned to her grandmother. "Let's go."

Gran stared at her. "Me?" she said.

"Yes, you. You put us into this mess. You get us out of it."

"But I didn't shoot nobody!"

"No, but you insisted on bringing the cats along, and now they've gone missing. So I personally hold you responsible."

"No fair," Gran muttered, but still proceeded in the direction of the cars. Time to go and wake up the neighbors!

CHAPTER 22

It wasn't the first time that we found ourselves in a position of captivity, but I still didn't much enjoy it. Especially since I had left the house with a certain reluctance, and only because Harriet had insisted I join them for cat choir. So now there was no cat choir, no nap time in my immediate future—only being locked up in some dank old farmhouse!

Johnny and Jerry had put us in some old barn that must have been where they kept the horses at one time, or the cows, for it was very smelly in there, and not very clean. At least they had put some food out for us in the form of a few pieces of sausage—or a lot of sausage. And even though sausage isn't exactly my favorite food, I still ate it with a certain relish. When you're hungry you can eat almost anything, as long as it's edible.

"I don't like it here, Max," said Dooley as he huddled close to me. We had found a spot on an old wooden crate that was more or less comfortable, and so we had settled in for the night.

"No, I don't like it very much either," I confessed.

Harriet and Brutus had decided that settling down was not in the cards for them, and had gone looking for an avenue of escape. But after they had done the rounds of the old barn, they had to admit defeat.

"I don't know," said Harriet after they joined us again, "but there doesn't seem to be a chance of escape here, you guys. Everything is locked up tight, and I don't see a way out."

"Not even a small hole?" I asked hopefully. "Or a crack in the roof?"

"Nothing," said Harriet. "We'll have to wait until we're saved by our humans—or until Johnny and Jerry grow a conscience and decide to let us out again."

"Fat chance," I said. "Those two are career crooks. They won't have a change of heart—ever."

"No, I guess not," said Brutus. "Otherwise they would have left this life of crime behind a long time ago."

Once upon a time, the two men had decided to walk the straight and narrow, but that hadn't lasted long. And now they seemed to have embraced their criminal true selves more wholeheartedly than ever.

"They must be paid a great deal of money for this," Brutus ventured. "Otherwise they wouldn't be doing it."

"I guess contract killers are highly sought after," I agreed. "Hence the high pay package."

I decided to close my eyes for a moment, eager to get some of that much-vaunted nap time I had been seeking for a while now. And as my friends did the same, I suddenly thought I heard voices. They seemed to be coming from behind us. And when I opened my eyes and glanced up, I saw that there was an opening in the wall behind us. It was a grille that covered some kind of ventilation shaft. "Look, you guys," I said. "I think that leads to the main farmhouse."

PURRFECT SPY

We all moved a little closer and huddled around the vent, listening carefully.

"I don't like this, Jerry," said Johnny.

"What don't you like?" said his partner in crime.

"Locking up those cats! You know they belong to Marge Poole, and we both like Marge Poole, don't we?"

"We sure do," Jerry agreed.

"So let's agree that we won't harm a hair on their heads, all right?"

"Agreed," said Jerry. "Marge doesn't deserve to have her cats involved in this mess."

"We should have used dynamite," Johnny grumbled. "That way we wouldn't have to keep going back there time after time, trying to get rid of this guy. He's so hard to kill."

"You can't throw sticks of dynamite at a police station, Johnny," Jerry argued. "It brings the entire structure down, and the police don't like that. They're attached to their precinct."

"I guess you're right. So what do you suggest we do?"

"It'll be hard to get at the guy now. So we must find a way to get close to him somehow."

"Let's talk to our contact again," Johnny suggested.

There was a pause, and then Jerry said, "Oh, hi, Maria. This is your Uncle Jerry again."

Harriet's eyes went wide. "You don't think... the dispatcher?"

"Possible," I admitted. It would explain how the crooks knew where Rogelio was.

The voice of the young woman sounded through the ventilation shaft loud and clear, and I immediately recognized it as belonging to the dispatcher we had spoken to earlier. Harriet was right. "Oh, hi, Uncle Jerry. Have you managed to get hold of Auntie Marlene yet?"

"No, I haven't been able to reach her."

"But didn't the lawyer tell you where she is?"

"I didn't have a chance to ask! When we arrived, a couple of crazies started shooting the place up."

"Oh, I know all about that!" said the young woman. "Things are nuts here right now!"

"But you're all right?"

"I'm fine. I was out in front when it happened, so they were nowhere near me."

"And the guy we want to talk to? Is he all right?"

"He is," said the dispatcher. "He's shaken but unharmed."

"Good," said Jerry. "That's great to hear. Do you think you could arrange a meeting?"

"Um… I guess that's going to be a little difficult at the moment? I mean, security is really tight right now, Uncle Jerry. The chief got the place locked down. Nobody is to go in or out."

"So you won't be able to smuggle me in?"

"Not a chance," said the girl. "I'm sorry."

"It's not your fault," said Jerry. "It's those crazy gunmen who ruined things for us." He sighed deeply. "I just wish I could have talked to the guy. It's your grandmother's legacy that's on the line, you know, so it's important."

"I know. But maybe you'll be able to talk to him once those gunmen have been arrested? I've heard the chief mention they're on to them. So it probably won't be long before Mr. Hartshorn can return to his office."

"Oh, so they're on to those gunmen, are they?" he asked casually.

"Yes, they are! Turns out a couple of cats managed to jump into their van, and now they're going to get a dog to trace those cats. As I understand it, the dog has done it before."

"That's great," said Jerry, but he didn't sound happy about

it, which was understandable. "How long before they find them, would you say?"

"A matter of hours," said the girl.

"Great," said Jerry. "That's just great." The moment he had disconnected, he cried, "Those stupid cats! They're going to get us caught—again!"

For a moment, the two crooks didn't speak, as they considered their options. Then Jerry said, "I'm afraid there's only one thing we can do."

"I know," said Johnny sadly.

"Are you gonna do it or do I have to?"

"I'll do it," said Johnny.

"Make it quick."

"Yes, Jer."

"And painless."

"Yes, Jer." He sighed deeply. "Poor cats. I kinda like them."

"They shouldn't have jumped into our van, buddy."

"Yeah, I guess they only got themselves to blame."

We all shared a look, and I think we were aware of the fate that awaited us.

Looked like we had finally reached the end of the road!

CHAPTER 23

"Max, I want you to know that it's been an honor to be your friend," said Dooley, a little tearfully I have to say.

"Buddy," I said, and I couldn't get the words out because of the big lump in my throat.

"I love you guys," said Harriet as she sniffled a little. "And to prove it to you, I'm going to sing you one final song. It's a power ballad and it reflects exactly how I feel about you." She took a deep breath, and before we could stop her, she had launched into a haunting rendition of *I Don't Want to Miss a Thing* by Aerosmith. It wasn't her usual genre, but she did it well—or at least she did it loud, and I guess that's what it's all about when you want to get into power ballad territory. You can miss a couple of notes but you have to hammer home the ones you hit.

She was still giving it her all when the door to the barn opened and a shadow fell across the four of us. Johnny stood there, large and threatening. He was lit up from behind by the light of a full moon, and I could see the knife glittering in his hand.

"I hope he does me first," said Brutus. "I really don't want to watch when he takes your lives, you guys." He pounded me on the back. "I love you, Max. I know we didn't always get along, but I consider you my best friend and one of the greatest cats that has ever lived, if not *the* greatest." He sniffed. "Max, you're the GOAT!"

Dooley glared at him. "Max is not a goat, Brutus! He's a cat!"

"I know he's a cat, buddy," said Brutus with a lopsided smile. "But he's also the Greatest Of All Time—the GOAT."

Dooley didn't seem to agree that Brutus was calling me a goat, but there was no more time for us to thresh this out, for Johnny was upon us. He had brought along a big burlap sack, and as he placed us all in the sack, I thought he would take us outside and do this in a quiet place. Or maybe he would simply drown us in the river? At any rate, I was resigned to my fate. I'd lived a long and full life with the best humans a cat can ever hope to have and the best friends.

"Okay, so shall I sing you one final song?" Harriet suggested.

"Mm, maybe we should enjoy these final moments in silence?" I suggested.

"I could sing something by Taylor Swift? Or Billie Eilish?"

Suddenly we heard Dooley murmur something. "Are you... praying, Dooley?" asked Brutus.

"I am, yes," said Dooley.

"For us to be saved?" I asked.

"No, for Harriet not to sing anymore," he said.

Harriet gave him a poke in the ribs. "Dooley! How can you say that!"

"It hurts my ears when you sing, Harriet!" he cried. "I know I've never said it before, but it does! My ears bleed when you sing! There, I've said it!"

"But Dooley! I thought you loved my singing! Max, you love my singing, don't you?"

"Well…"

"These are our final moments, Max," Dooley reminded me. "You should be honest and tell Harriet the truth."

He was right. If you can't tell the truth in your final moments before you face certain death, when can you? And so I steeled myself. "Okay, so I don't really enjoy your singing either, Harriet. Like Dooley says, it hurts my ears. A lot."

"But Max!" Harriet cried. "You never said! How about you, pookie?"

"Um…." said Pookie.

"Not you, too! I don't believe this! You've all been lying to me all this time?"

"We haven't been lying," I said. "We just haven't told you the truth. There's a difference."

"Max is right," said Brutus. "We would never lie to you, buttercup. But sometimes we don't tell you the truth—just to spare your feelings, you know."

"Oh. My. God! This is the worst day of my life!"

"Yeah, it's not the greatest day of my life either," I said. All I could think about was that either I was going to have my throat slit or I was about to drown. Neither option held a lot of appeal to me.

The bag was swinging from side to side as Johnny carried us on his back. Moments later we were put down on a hard surface, and I thought this was the moment. The moment he was going to take out his big knife and do his worst. But instead we heard a door slam and a car engine turning over. Before long, we were mobile again, rocking and bumping over uneven terrain, just like before.

"I don't understand," said Brutus. "Where is he taking us?"

"Maybe he wants to drown us in the lake?" I suggested.

"But I don't *want* to drown in the lake!" said Dooley.

"I don't want to drown, period," said Brutus dryly.

The trip seemed endless, and then all of a sudden it ended. The van pulled to a stop and the door was opened, and the bag grabbed again before being placed down. There was a sort of scratchy noise and then the bag fell away, and we found ourselves blinking. Johnny stared down at us and gave us a smile. Then he waved. "See you around, little buddies."

When we looked around, we saw that he had dropped us off in front of our own home! And then he got back into the van and took off in a cloud of dust and exhaust fumes—not a fan of electric vehicles, this one, but of sturdy old diesel.

"But… I thought he was going to murder us," said Harriet.

Instead, we watched him take off at a fast clip, and turn the corner at the end of the street with screeching tires before disappearing from view. We all yipped in jubilation, but then all of a sudden I became aware of Harriet looking at us in a not-so-friendly way, tapping the tarmac with her front paw.

"So you don't like my singing, huh!" she said in a snappish sort of tone.

Uh-oh!

CHAPTER 24

As we stood there, wondering how to escape Harriet's ire, a fleet of police vehicles came driving up and parked in front of the house next door. We watched as Chase got out of one of the vehicles, accompanied by Uncle Alec, Odelia, and several officers. They hurried up to the Trapper place and applied their fingers to the buzzer.

"Why are they calling on the Trappers in the middle of the night?" asked Brutus. "Don't they know they're fast asleep?"

"Maybe they want to ask them an urgent question?" Dooley suggested.

"Or maybe Ted has been a naughty boy," Brutus said. "And now they've come to arrest him."

"Ted may not be a very nice man sometimes," I said, "but I can't imagine he would ever knowingly break the law."

"No, he definitely is the epitome of the law-abiding citizen," Brutus agreed.

"Look, you can try and distract my attention all you want," said Harriet. "But it won't work, you know. You've all been busted. You don't like my singing and yet you pretended all this time that you did! So who else doesn't like my singing? Tell me!"

When the ringing of the bell didn't work, Chase used his fist to bang on the door, while Uncle Alec used *his* fist to bang on the front window. And when that didn't produce the desired effect, Odelia started yelling, "Police! Open the door!"

"Looks like it's really urgent," said Brutus.

"Must be important," said Dooley.

"Maybe they urgently need an accountant?" I suggested.

Brutus laughed. "An accountancy emergency. Good one, Max."

We saw that another car had driven up. It was Gran's little red Peugeot, and as the old lady parked behind the fleet of police vehicles, she and Scarlett got out and joined the growing throng of people on the Trappers' doorstep desiring to speak with the couple.

"Let us in!" Gran demanded as she, too, applied her fist to the door.

"Let us handle this, Vesta," said Chase.

"But they're mine, too, you know," said Gran.

We all shared a look, and even Harriet had forgotten about her beef with us. "I wonder if this is connected to the shooting," she said. "Do you think Ted was involved somehow?"

"I doubt it," I said. "Why would Ted hire two crooks to shoot up the police station? It doesn't make sense."

"I've always suspected that man of having hidden depths," said Brutus. "It's in his face, you know. He seems too nice. Exactly the kind of person who's hiding a deep, dark secret."

"So you think Ted killed Prince Abdullah and is now trying to get rid of the man's lawyer?" I asked.

"And why not? Maybe the prince is a client of Ted's accountancy firm and they fell out over some tax issue?"

It was definitely the most ridiculous thing I'd ever heard,

but since I didn't want to insult Brutus's intelligence by voicing this determination, I simply kept my mouth firmly shut.

The Trappers must finally have understood that there was someone out there who wanted to talk to them, for the light upstairs suddenly flicked on, then the light downstairs, and the door opened a crack and a pair of suspicious eyes peered out through the opening. "What's this all about?" asked a sleepy Ted.

"Police," said Chase, flashing his badge. "We need to borrow your dog, Ted."

"My dog? What do you want to borrow my dog for?"

"The cats have been abducted," Odelia explained. "Rufus needs to track them down."

"But... Rufus isn't a police dog," said Ted, having opened the door fully and revealing himself to be wearing nice-looking pajamas with blue Smurfs and ditto fluffy slippers. His hair was tousled and his eyes half-lidded, but otherwise he looked his usual self—not the crime lord that Brutus had him pegged as.

"Rufus knows the cats," said Odelia. "And he's found them before."

It was at this moment that we felt we should probably let our presence be known, to avoid further complications and embarrassing situations. And so we stepped to the fore to join the small throng on the Trapper doorstep.

"Odelia," I said. "We're fine."

But Odelia paid me no mind at all. Instead, she addressed Ted in a rather recalcitrant way. "Look, if you don't want to lend Rufus to us, I'm afraid we'll have to confiscate him."

"You can't do that," said Ted. "Rufus is my dog and you can't have him."

"Odelia," said Harriet. "We're right here, honey."

But Odelia was so caught up in her argument with Ted

that she didn't even notice us. "We are taking that dog," she said, "whether you like it or not!"

"And I'm telling you that you're *not* taking him!" Ted yelled back.

Marcie had also joined her husband in the door opening. She also looked sleepy and had probably just woken up from a pleasant dream. "What's with all the noise?"

"They want to take Rufus!" Ted cried indignantly. "Just like that!"

"What? You can't take our dog!" said Marcie, immediately up in arms about Odelia's request.

"Odelia?" said Dooley. "You don't have to bother Rufus, you know. We're perfectly fine."

"We were abducted," I said. "But Johnny brought us back."

"Even though we thought for a moment that he was going to murder us and bury our bodies in the woods," said Brutus.

Finally, someone in the small entourage must have noticed us, for an officer tapped on Chase's shoulder. "Sir? Are these the cats that you're looking for?"

Chase looked down, and when he saw us, did a double take. "But... where did you come from all of a sudden?" He then tapped Odelia on the shoulder.

"Not now, Chase," said the reporter. "I'm talking to Ted and Marcie."

"But, babe," he said.

"I said not now!" she yelled, and I saw that her face was a little red, usually a sign she's feeling worked up. It certainly was balm to our wounded souls that our human cared for us so much she would be willing to go to bat for us and engage the Trappers in this argument.

"Give me that dog!" she yelled.

"Never!" Ted yelled back.

"It's our constitutional right not to hand our dog over to the police!" Marcie added for good measure.

"Last time I looked we weren't living in a police state!" Ted said. "So you can't have Rufus and that's my final word!"

And with this, he stepped back and slammed the door in Odelia's face.

"Babe!" said Chase urgently.

"What!" she yelled and turned to face him and give him a piece of her mind. Which is when she saw me, hoisted up in her husband's arms, and waving at her from my pleasant vantage point. I always enjoy being picked up by Chase, since he's so big and strong and he makes us feel safe in his arms.

Odelia's jaw actually dropped. "But… I don't understand."

"We were kidnapped," I explained. "And then let go again."

"It's Johnny and Jerry," said Brutus. "They're the ones behind the shootings." And he told her where the criminal duo had held us captive before setting us free again.

Odelia's anger morphed into an expression of pure delight, and then all of a sudden she started crying! Big tears trickled down her cheeks and she was sobbing like a baby!

"Odd," said Dooley. "I thought she'd be happy to see us, and instead she's sad!"

"She's so happy she's sad," I explained.

Dooley shook his head. "Humans. So hard to read."

And wasn't that the truth? Sometimes they cry because they're happy and other times they laugh when they're angry or sad. Tough to know what's going on! But at any rate, Odelia was overjoyed to see us, for she crouched down and hugged us all in turn, then pulled us in for a group hug. Then she rose to her feet and whispered something in her husband's ear.

His face grew hard. "We're moving out," he told his officers. "New information has come to light. The men who shot up the police station are Johnny Carew and Jerry Vale." He made a circular motion in the air with his fingers, and before we knew what was going on, he was hurrying back to his squad car, and so were the other officers.

Odelia chose to stay behind. She was smiling now, and was holding me so tight I had trouble breathing.

"Can you… ease up on the hug… a smidgen?" I asked. It wouldn't do for me to escape Jerry and Johnny's clutches only to be smothered to death by my own human.

"Oh, I'm sorry," she said. "I'm so happy you guys are safe! I was so worried!"

"They would never hurt us," said Brutus confidently, even though a short while ago he was sure our final hour had struck. "Johnny and Jerry may be a lot of things, but they're not cat killers."

"Whatever they are, we'll know soon," said Odelia. "Chase has gone to arrest them. Let's hope they haven't fled the scene. And then maybe we'll know why they tried to shoot Rogelio."

"And if they're the ones that killed Prince Abdullah," I added. I couldn't believe they would do such a thing, as mostly they're small-time criminals, not murderers. But then sometimes this kind of criminal behavior is like going to McDonald's. You start with a bag of French fries and before you know it you're scarfing down one Happy Meal after another.

"So… are we going to borrow Ted and Marcie's dog or not?" asked Gran, who hadn't really been following closely. "I mean, if you want me to go and get him, I can, you know."

"You don't have to get Rufus, Gran," said Odelia. "We've got the cats back so everything is fine now."

"If you're sure. I mean, I got nothing against Ted and Marcie, but when the police show up in the middle of the night, accompanied by the neighborhood watch, asking their assistance in a matter of life and death, they should comply, you know. Do their civic duty. So if you want me to get

Rufus, I will. And if they protest, slap a pair of handcuffs on them. That'll teach 'em."

"It's fine, Vesta," said Scarlett. "The cats are back, so we don't need Rufus anymore."

"People like the Trappers should be taught a lesson. A night in the pokey will make them think twice about refusing to assist the police and the neighborhood watch in their inquiries. And besides, we're their neighbors. You should always be neighborly to your neighbors."

"It's all right, Vesta," said Scarlett as she placed an arm around her friend's shoulder. "Everything is fine now."

It had certainly been an eventful night, and for Chase the night wasn't over yet, and neither was it for Uncle Alec. Which is why I was surprised when Harriet said, "Well? Are we going to cat choir or not?"

"You still want to go?" asked Brutus. "After everything that happened?"

"Of course! At least Shanille appreciates my singing. Unlike the three of you—who have revealed yourselves as my worst critics!"

Looked like she hadn't forgotten about our critique on her singing talent.

And she wouldn't let us forget it either!

CHAPTER 25

When we finally set out for the park, Rufus came tripping after us, and so did Fifi, our other neighbor's dog.

"What was that all about?" asked Rufus. "Did Odelia need me for something?"

"She needed you to find us," I explained. "But since we were returned home in one piece, in the end it wasn't necessary."

"Oh, but I would have loved to find you," said Rufus.

"You were missing?" asked Fifi.

"We were abducted," I said. "By Johnny and Jerry."

"Not again!" said Rufus, who had gone down that road with us before.

"Yeah, they were up to their old tricks again," I said.

"In their defense, this time they didn't actually abduct us," said Brutus. "We jumped into their van when they weren't looking, and since they have been bad boys again, they didn't see any other solution but to lock us up so we wouldn't tell our humans what they've been up to."

"I still don't understand why Johnny would let us go like

that," said Harriet. "He must have known that we would blab to our humans the first chance we got."

"They probably left that farmhouse the moment he got back," I said. "No way they would sit there and wait to be arrested. They're not the smartest criminals, but they're not that dumb."

"Rufus, I'm going to ask you a question," said Harriet. "And I want you to answer me sincerely and honestly, is that understood?"

"Of course, Harriet," said Rufus. "What do you want to know?"

"You've heard me sing, right?"

"Oh, lots of times," said Rufus. "And you have a lovely singing voice. Very… clear."

She perked up considerably. "So would you say that you enjoy my singing? That you actually like to listen to me sing?"

"Of course," said the big sheepdog. "Who wouldn't? Your singing is like listening to a church bell. It's very loud and very clear." He smiled. "I like loud and clear voices. Not like those modern singers who mumble and you practically can't make out what they're singing."

Harriet seemed extremely pleased with this compliment from an unsuspected source. She turned to Fifi, and the latter already knew the way the wind was blowing, for she held up a paw. "Yes, I like your singing, Harriet," said the little Yorkie. "It's just like Rufus said: you sing very loud and clear, and I enjoy that very much. Like the sound of a car horn, you know. Or a fire truck. You hear it and immediately you're like: that's Harriet singing. Unmistakable."

Harriet didn't seem entirely sure if she had just been given a compliment or not, but decided to accept it anyway. "Why, thanks, Fifi," she said, and cast a meaningful look in my direction. "See, Max? There are pets who appreciate true art. You could learn a thing or two from Fifi and Rufus."

"Oh, but I agree that your singing is very loud and very clear," I said. It just wasn't a lot of fun to listen to. Just like Fifi had indicated, it was like listening to a car horn or a fire truck. It's distinctive, and it certainly has its purposes, but you can't listen to it for hours at a time.

We had arrived at the park, and Harriet immediately went in search of Shanille, the choir conductor, to ask her how she felt about her qualities as a singer. Which just goes to show: even when you think you're about to die, you better hold back on blurting out those truth bombs.

I joined Kingman, who was standing on the sidelines for a change and wasn't the center of attention like he usually was. "Everything all right, buddy?" I asked.

"I can't complain, Max," he said, and I got a feeling he was about to do just that. "The thing is that I've been eating the same kibble for a week, and I'm getting a little bored, you know."

"Wilbur keeps feeding you the same stuff?" I asked.

"He thinks it's all different brands he's giving me to try out, but when you get right down to it, it all tastes the same. Just like that kibble you guys tried today, remember?"

"But that *was* the same kibble," I said.

"No, it wasn't. It was different, but in the end it was the same. Very odd."

"Maybe it's all the same company? And they simply use different labels?" I suggested.

"It's possible. I don't like it, Max. If they put a different label on it and use different packaging, you expect there to be a difference, right? But there isn't. It's all the same. Identical."

He had certainly changed his tune, as he had insisted before there was a big difference between Brand A and

Brand B. Having snacked on the stuff all day, he had come around to my way of thinking.

"Max!" said Dooley as he came hurrying up to us. "Come quick. It's Harriet. She's picking a fight with Shanille!"

"Oh, dear," I said, and hurried after my friend. It was as he had said: Harriet and Shanille were at daggers drawn for some reason.

"I'm the finest singer this choir has ever had," said Harriet. "And I'll prove it right now!"

"Oh, please don't, Harriet," said Shanille. "Let's just get to our rehearsal, shall we?"

Harriet looked around at the other members of the choir, who had all gathered around the two ladies. "I'm going to sing a song—any song—and you have to give me either a thumbs up or a thumbs down. The majority will decide whether I stay on as lead soprano or I quit the choir. Is that clear?"

There were loud cheers, as cats all love a spectacle, and this was definitely going to make a big splash.

"Okay, give me a song to sing," she told Shanille.

The choir leader rolled her eyes. "Look, all I said was that there is always room for improvement. You're an excellent singer but you're not perfect. But then nobody is!"

"Just give me a song, Shanille!" Harriet demanded.

"Okay, so how about *Nothing's Gonna Stop Us Now?*" said Shanille.

Harriet smiled. "You're on, sister! Oh, you are so going to regret taking on this wager!"

"But I didn't take on any wager!" Shanille protested. "I just want to get back to our regular rehearsal. Can we not stop this silly nonsense?"

In response Harriet opened her mouth and started wailing *Nothing's Gonna Stop Us Now* to the excitement of all those gathered around. She certainly put the power in the word power ballad, I thought, as the hair on the back of my neck rose from her rendition of the popular song. When she paused to take a breath, plenty of thumbs went up—and down—and as she looked around, I could tell that she was a little disappointed that not all thumbs pointed to the sky but that a lot of them pointed to the ground. "Okay, give me another song!" she snapped.

Shanille sighed. "Fine. How about *It Must Have Been Love?*"

Harriet did as the choir leader suggested, and expertly massacred this lovely song in her own typical fashion. This time more thumbs pointed up than down, and it was clear that this pleased her to no end. "Another one!" she demanded. "Three out of three!"

"Um… try *Heaven,* the Bryan Adams song," said Shanille.

And as our friend started belting out the opening notes of the famous tune, I could see plenty of cats grimacing a little as their eardrums were being subjected to a particularly brutal treatment. Several shoes started landing all around us, proving that the park's neighbors had also joined the wager and were voting with footwear instead of their thumbs. I didn't know how to interpret this, though. Was a thrown shoe a thumb down or up? Hard to determine! This time the number of thumbs pointing down were in the majority, causing Harriet to be faced with quite the head-scratcher. Was she in with a chance or out on her ear?

She turned to Brutus. "Did you keep count, smoochie poo?"

"I did, as a matter of fact," said her loyal and faithful mate. "I counted more thumbs up than down—plenty more, my precious angel."

Harriet shook her fist and did a little victory dance on the spot. "See!" she told Shanille. "I'm popular—the most popular soprano this choir has ever had!"

"You're the only soprano this choir has ever had," said Shanille, never one to mince words. "And I never said you weren't good, Harriet. I just said there's always room for improvement."

"You're wrong, Shanille," Harriet snapped. She tossed her head back dramatically. "You can't improve on perfection and I'm the living proof!"

CHAPTER 26

At the breakfast table, last night's events were the sole topic of conversation. As I had expected, Johnny and Jerry had long fled the scene when the police finally arrived, and there was no way of knowing where they were holed up now or whether they would try to get rid of Rogelio Hartshorn again. The man had been transferred from his prison cell to a safe location outside of town. He was, in fact, staying with Charlene Butterwick and Uncle Alec now, but only for the time being, until a suitable location could be found for the unfortunate lawyer.

Jerry's niece Maria Cannon hadn't been told where the lawyer was, for fear she would blurt it out to her uncle. Uncle Alec decided not to suspend or punish her, but he did have a long talk with the young woman, and explained to her a thing or two about practicing discretion, especially to the likes of Jerry Vale, who was a convicted criminal. She was absolutely mortified when she understood that her uncle had used her to get information on a target, the poor girl.

"I asked Rogelio again why he thought he was being targeted," said Chase as he bit down into a sandwich smeared with a brown substance I could only assume was Nutella. "And he swore he has no idea. And I believe him. Whoever it is that wants him dead, he honestly has no clue, and neither do we," he added on a sour note. He took a sip from his piping hot coffee and directed a loving look across the breakfast table at his daughter Grace. "Looking forward to another day at the daycare, sweetie?"

"Oh, absolutely," said Grace. "Yesterday, Timmy and I discovered a fun new game. We dunk all the Legos in a tub with warm water and soap. Then we let them dry, and it's so much fun to see other kids try to pick them up but they can't because they're all slippery. So much fun!"

"That's great, sweetie," said Chase who, as usual, hadn't understood her babbling at all. Oddly enough, only us cats can.

"You shouldn't do that, Grace," said Harriet. "It's not nice to the other kids—or the teacher, who has to rinse those Legos again and then dry them."

"But soap is good for you," said the little girl. "Everybody knows that soap is a wonderful substance and we can never have enough of it."

I shook my head. "I hope at least you don't eat the soap?"

"Of course not," she said. But then frowned. "Though I was wondering... if soap is so good for you, maybe we should eat it? To clean our insides, I mean? So they're nice and shiny?"

"Please don't," said Harriet. "You'll get sick if you do."

"I'm not *stupid*, Harriet," said Grace. "I wouldn't try to *eat* a bar of soap. But I could feed it to my friends, and see what happens. And if they are okay, I can try it myself, you know."

It was exactly the same logic Gran used from time to time, which just goes to show that certain habits transfer from generation to generation. Gran entered the house at that moment through the sliding glass door and searched around eagerly. When she spotted Harriet, she smiled. "Can you come with me for a moment, Harriet? I need you for an experiment."

Harriet was pleased to be selected and immediately followed Gran out of the house and into the backyard.

"What about that older couple?" asked Odelia. "Andy and Brandy Pettey?"

"The Petteys are innocent," said Chase. "Nothing to do with this whole sordid business whatsoever. I let them walk last night after the shooting." He grimaced. "Though it looks as if being locked up and shot at didn't sit well with them, and they're lawyering up. Threatening to take us to court for wrongful arrest and putting their lives in jeopardy. They also said that Hampton Cove is going to the dogs and want to go to the press with the whole story."

"Looks like some bad publicity is coming our way then," said Odelia, who didn't look even remotely bothered. Plenty of people have tried to sue the Hampton Cove police for wrongful arrest, and only in extremely rare cases have the judges gone along with them. Chase doesn't arrest people simply because he doesn't like their faces or because they've rubbed him the wrong way. He always has a good reason, and the judges can appreciate that.

Though in the case of the old couple, it was true that he hadn't had a lot to go on. Apart from the fact that they were embroiled in some kind of fracas with the bug spray people.

"And Carlos and Mindy?" I asked. "Are they still suspects in the murder of the prince?"

"Oh, absolutely," said Odelia. "The gun that was used to murder Prince Abdullah was found hidden away inside their mock-up. And even though they claim they had nothing to do with it, they were at the scene, and so they had opportunity and means to murder the man."

"But what about motive?" I asked. "Why would they murder a customer?"

Odelia nodded. "That's the part that we haven't been able to figure out. And also, the role that Johnny Carew and Jerry Vale play in this whole business."

"They must have been hired by Perks and Horsefield," said Chase. "To get rid of the lawyer."

"But why?" I asked.

Odelia shook her head. "No idea." She gave me a hopeful look. "You wouldn't have some bright idea, would you, Max?"

"No idea," I confessed. It certainly was a most baffling case. A prince being murdered, a lawyer targeted, and the only people locked up were a couple of bug spray salespeople. Things did not look good for the investigation. "Did you find out more about the prince?" I asked. "Possible enemies? If Johnny and Jerry had been paid to get rid of the lawyer, maybe Carlos Perks had also been paid to provide the same service in regards to the prince. There was that message written on his mirror, remember?" I had told her all about that threatening message.

"Well, it all gets a little strange from that point onward," said Odelia. "Prince Abdullah was traveling alone, which is unusual for a member of the royal house of Abou-Yamen, as they always travel with an entourage, security people, and such. Also, when we contacted the embassy of Abou-Yamen, they weren't very eager to supply us with more information in connection with the prince. They didn't even want to give us the prince's biography, though we have found some information about him online, most notably his Wikipedia page. Which tells us that he is married with three kids, all of them living in Abou-Yamen. And that he's one of the crown prince's sons—the crown prince has nine sons and three daughters. But apart from that, we don't know why he was traveling to the United States all by himself to buy bug spray."

"Maybe the country of Abou-Yamen is having a lot of trouble with bugs?" I ventured.

"Yes, but he doesn't have a connection with the Minister of Agriculture, so his mission wasn't officially sanctioned or approved by the ministry or the king of Abou-Yamen."

"Looks like he was traveling as a private person," said Chase. "Not as an official representative of his country or the royal house to which he belongs."

"Could it be that he wanted to buy that bug spray for his own personal use?" I asked. "Maybe he owns a lot of land and he wanted to keep it free of bugs?"

"Hard to tell," said Odelia as she put a spoonful of cereal into her mouth. "Uncle Alec says the only way to find out what the prince was doing here would be to travel to Abou-Yamen and talk to his family. But he doesn't feel that the expenditure is justified, especially since we have two suspects in jail right now that he feels are almost certainly the prince's killers."

"And then there's the estate business," said Chase. "Why did the prince arrange a meeting with an estate lawyer? If it was in connection to his personal estate, wouldn't he consult with an estate lawyer in his own country? American estate law is different from Abou-Yamen laws, so whatever advice he was going to get wouldn't be applicable in his situation anyway."

Odelia threw down her napkin. "I'm going over to talk to Rogelio again. Wanna join me?"

"Absolutely," I said. The more I dug into this mystery, the less I understood what was going on, so I figured that I just had to keep collecting more information. Maybe something would jump out at me that would make it all make sense at some point.

Just then, Harriet came staggering into the living room. She looked a little discombobulated.

"She zapped me!" she cried indignantly. "She actually zapped me with that weed killer!"

"Not weed killer," said Gran, who was right behind her and was holding a can that looked awfully familiar. She held it up with a triumphant smile. "It's bug spray, and it's going to make us all richer than Jesus!"

"Croesus," I murmured, figuring Jesus had never featured on the Forbes rich list.

"What is that?" asked Odelia, who is extremely protective of her cats. She got up. "What did you do to Harriet?"

Gran displayed a mysterious smile as she shook the can. "Harriet is going to be pregnant—so you better get that notebook out, honey, so you can write about this miracle of nature!"

"Did you spray this stuff on Harriet?" asked Odelia, her voice going a little shrill. She tried to grab the can from her grandmother. "Give me that!"

"Never!" Gran cried, and promptly sprinted in the direction of the great outdoors, evading her granddaughter's attempts to snatch that spray from her hands. "This is history in the making and you better write down every detail! It's the scoop of a lifetime—get off me!"

"If you used that bug spray on Harriet, I swear to God I'm going to…" Odelia began, and didn't finish the sentence, though it was clear that what she had in mind for her grandmother wasn't to be classified under the heading of granddaughterly love. Quite the contrary. It might even get her sent to prison. "Get back here!"

But Gran quickly threw the can in the direction of Blake's Field before Odelia could grab it. The old lady took a stance like a professional pitcher and hurled that can out so far that it would take a miracle to find it out there unless you knew where to look. She then stood in front of her granddaughter, hands on hips. "You're a pretty lousy reporter!" she said accusingly. "You can't even see an amazing scoop when it hits you in the snoot!"

"You just poisoned my cat!" Odelia said.

"I did no such thing!"

"I'm taking her to the vet," said Odelia, scooping the white Persian into her arms. "And if she gets sick…"

"She won't get sick," said Gran. "But she will get pregnant," she promised. "Just you wait and see."

"Nuts," said Odelia, and was off with Harriet in her arms.

"I don't want to *go* to the vet!" Harriet lamented.

"Too bad, 'cause you're gonna!" said Odelia.

And since we couldn't possibly let Harriet go through this ordeal alone, the three of us followed after Odelia as she hurried out of the house.

CHAPTER 27

As we sat waiting in Vena's waiting room, while Harriet was being given the once-over by the vet, our friend Norm came buzzing in. "Hey, you guys," he said, looking a little downcast, I thought.

"Norm," I said. "How are things in the world of superflies?"

My words had been chosen as an attempt to cheer him up, but they didn't have that effect. On the contrary, his wings drooped as he selected a spot on a seat next to us. "It's Norma," he said. "She put her foot down this time. If I don't provide her with offspring, she'll go and find herself a different husband. One who will fulfill his marital duties with speed and effectiveness."

"But I thought you said you were going to embrace the life of the paterfamilias?"

"I know, but I'm having second thoughts."

Sounded to me as if he was having third thoughts, or maybe even fourth or fifth. Then again, becoming a father is a big deal, and a lot of men find it hard to take that step as it is bound to change their lives forever—and quite irrevocably, too.

"But your friend the cockroach—didn't he tell you how wonderful it is to be a dad?"

"He didn't. He told me how rotten it is."

"Harriet is pregnant," Dooley said.

"We don't know that, Dooley," Brutus hissed. Clearly, he wasn't very keen on becoming a father either. When push came to shove, being a dad was a scary proposition.

"No, but she is," said Dooley. "Gran says she's pregnant, and Gran knows, since she's been pregnant herself, so she knows the signs."

"Gran zapped Harriet with that same bug spray that Tex used on the bugs in our backyard, the same used at the hotel," I told Norm. "And since it seems to have led to a proliferation of those bugs, she's hoping that it will do the same thing with Harriet and pretty soon the world will be full of little Harriets."

Norm laughed. "Oh, Max. Do you really think you can create kittens by using bug spray on a cat? That's very naive, even for you."

"I never said I believed her," I said. Though obviously my friends all did. Except for Norm, but then he was a wise old fly.

"Look, do you love Norma?" I asked.

"Of course I do. She's the love of my life. The one fly for me, you know."

"Then I think you should have a little faith and go for it, buddy."

"But I have no idea how to be a dad," he said. "I mean, not the first clue."

"Just wing it," was Brutus's advice. "I don't know the first thing about being a dad either, and I'm scared to death that Vena will come walking out of that examination room and tell us it's a boy, but that doesn't matter one bit. Just do what feels right in your heart. At the end of the day that's all any of us can do. Give it our all." He glanced nervously at the door to Vena's inner realm, expecting the vet to come charging out and holding up a kitten, though I could have told him that it didn't work like that.

"Yeah, I guess you're right," said Norm. He seemed to relax a little. "Say, I saw that the killers of the prince are locked up in jail? Good job, you guys. I told you they did it, didn't I?"

"You certainly did, Norm," I said. "You called it."

"What can I say? I'm an ace detective." And with these words, he was off again, possibly to give the good news to Norma that he had thought things through and he wanted to be her baby daddy after all.

"So romantic, isn't it, Max?" said Dooley with a sigh. "Norm is going to be a daddy!"

"Absolutely," I said. "And I'm sure he'll be a great daddy, too."

"Will I be a great daddy, Max?" asked Brutus nervously.

"Of course you will!" I said. "You're a wonderful person, Brutus, and any kid would be lucky to have you as their daddy."

"I would have you as my daddy, Brutus," said Dooley.

Brutus gave him a strange look. "Okay. That's good to know."

Dooley patted him on the back. "Daddy Brutus."

The big black cat winced. "It'll take some getting used to."

Just then, the doors to the examination room opened and Vena appeared, along with Odelia, who was carrying Harriet in her arms. Vena was saying something, and Odelia was listening intently. Harriet not so much. She looked as if she still wasn't feeling well.

"How are you, sugar biscuit?" asked Brutus solicitously.

"Nauseous," said Harriet.

"That's to be expected," said Dooley. "A lot of pregnant ladies feel nauseous in the first couple of weeks of their pregnancy."

Harriet produced a tiny burp. "God, I feel awful."

"What did Vena say?" asked Brutus.

"Is it a boy or a girl?" asked Dooley.

"Neither," said Harriet. "It's a bad case of poisoning, and I need to detox for a while. She's given me some pills that should make me feel better real soon. Though they haven't kicked in yet, so there's always hoping they will soon."

"Poisoning?" asked Brutus. "I don't understand."

"What did you expect would happen when I got zapped with bug spray, sparky star? That stuff can't be good for you."

"But... I thought Gran said—"

"The lady is nuts, all right? She's always been certifiable and the older she gets, the worse she seems to get. Vena even told Odelia that maybe she should have her checked out for signs of dementia. I mean, who zaps their cat with bug spray and expects her to become pregnant?"

"Yeah, I guess when you put it like that," said Brutus doubtfully. He scratched his head. "So... I'm not going to be a daddy?"

"No, you're not," said Harriet. "And I just hope this whole bug spray incident hasn't affected my voice. Cause if it has, there will be hell to pay, I can tell you that right now!" She turned to me. "Give me a song, Max. Quick. Do it now."

"Um... *Total Eclipse of the Heart* by Bonnie Tyler?"

She nodded. "Give me a minute." She produced a few more burps, then started belting out Bonnie Tyler's biggest hit, a classic from the eighties. When we all covered our ears, and so did Vena, she smiled. "Looks like I've still got it."

CHAPTER 28

Now that Odelia had ascertained that Harriet wasn't pregnant—and also that she would live—she steered her car in the direction of the home of her aunt Charlene and Uncle Alec, not all that far from where we ourselves live. On the drive over, she peppered us with questions in connection to the bug spray that Gran had grand designs for, and when we told her that she planned to use it on women who were having trouble getting pregnant, a sort of mulish look came over her that I didn't like to see. I had a feeling that very soon now Gran would discover that she wasn't the only person in the family who was capable of putting her foot down.

She parked her car across the street from Charlene's house, and we all got out. Harriet was still a little unsteady on her feet, and so Odelia picked her up and carried her over.

"I'm so sorry this happened to you, honey," said Odelia.

"I'll be fine," said Harriet. "At least I can still sing. That's the most important thing. I haven't lost my voice."

Odelia smiled. "I don't think you will ever lose your voice. That voice of yours is unique."

"No, but there have been singers who have lost their voice," Harriet said. "Like Julie Andrews, for instance. And it's such a pity for she had such an amazing voice."

"That's true," said Odelia. She placed Harriet down for a moment and peered in through the window next to the front door. When Charlene appeared, she waved at her, and the mayor immediately came to open the door.

"Oh, hey, honey," said Charlene, and kissed her niece on the cheek. "I see you've brought your cats. How are they?"

"They've been through the wars," said Odelia. "First that kidnapping last night, and now Gran got it into her head that it would be a good idea to use bug spray on Harriet to get her pregnant."

Charlene laughed an incredulous laugh. "You're kidding."

"I'm not," Odelia assured her. "I didn't catch her in time, or I would have stopped her, of course. But I've just been to see Vena, and she thinks she'll be fine. Just a mild case of poisoning, but nothing that will have any lasting effect. Can I come in?"

"Oh, I'm so sorry!" said Charlene and stepped aside to let us all in. On the couch, we saw Rogelio reading a magazine. He looked up when he saw us and smiled. "Oh, hi there. So we meet again."

"I'm sorry to bother you again, Mr. Hartshorn," said Odelia. "But I wanted to ask you a few more questions, if I may."

"Absolutely," he said. "So have you found those men who shot at me?"

"No, they got away, I'm afraid," she said. "But at least now we know who they are, even if we don't know who hired them to try and kill you."

"It's still inconceivable to me that someone out there would want me dead," he said. "I mean, this is definitely a first for any estate lawyer, I would say. This isn't the kind of profession parents warn their kids about. More like they're over the moon when you tell them you want to be a lawyer. Great job security, financial benefits—and you may get shot at repeatedly by a couple of gangsters."

Odelia had taken a seat next to the man while Charlene disappeared into the kitchen. Her husband presumably had left for work, and so it was just us in the house—which is large and very modern, with plenty of glass and steel and concrete, but not in a cold and unpleasant way. We had stayed there before, so we considered Charlene's home our home away from home and were happy to find ourselves on familiar ground for a change. Mostly Odelia conducts these interviews on the premises, and often it's not what one expects: either more luxurious and outrageously opulent, or downright dilapidated and run down. This was neither, just a cozy little home designed for regular people like Charlene and Uncle Alec.

"Okay, so we've been in touch with the Abou-Yamen embassy," said Odelia. "And they weren't very helpful, I have to say. They didn't want to answer most of our questions, and so we still don't know a great deal about Prince Abdullah. Most of what we know is what we found on the internet, in fact, which is crazy when you come to think about it."

"I'm afraid I don't know all that much about the man myself, Mrs. Kingsley," said the lawyer.

"Odelia, please. After all that we've been through, I think it's safe to say we're on a first-name basis."

"Okay, fine," he said with a smile. "As I told you, I never met the man face to face. We talked on the phone, and we set up our appointment, but apart from that, I don't know more than what you do. Like you, I Googled him, of course, as it's not every day that an actual prince requests a meeting. But I expected him to supply me with the information I needed when he dropped by for our meeting—which as we know now never took place."

"All I know is that he's married with three kids—all of whom are living in Abou-Yamen. And that it's highly unusual for a member of the Abou-Yamen royal family to travel without an entourage or security detail."

"Yes, I can see that," said the lawyer.

"Also, the couple we have in prison right now, on suspicion of the prince's murder, told us that he didn't want to meet them in the hotel conference room as he was afraid it was bugged. He wanted to meet them in his suite where they could talk in private. Does that ring a bell?"

The lawyer nodded thoughtfully as a deep groove appeared between his brows. "It does, actually. I suggested we meet at the office, but he said he preferred we meet in a public place. He actually wanted to meet at the mall. Which I thought was a little strange."

"And you have no idea why he was so adamant not to meet at your office?"

The groove deepened as the man dug into his recollections. "Um… I seem to remember that he said it was safer for him to meet in a public environment, where we wouldn't be overheard. It all sounded a little James Bond to me, to be honest. But then I guess if you're a prince of a royal house you're entitled to a touch of eccentricity. And also, considering my line of work, whatever he wanted to see me about would have required the necessary discretion. We are dealing with inheritance matters, which are always very delicate."

"Yes, I can see that," said Odelia. "And I've read online that the grandfather of Prince Abdullah is old and poorly, so maybe Prince Abdullah was expecting him not to live much longer and wanted to discuss his possible inheritance with you."

"It's possible."

"Is there any reason you can think of why he wouldn't consult an estate lawyer in his own country, one who is more familiar with local law, and instead wanted an American lawyer?"

"The principles of estate law are similar in different jurisdictions, even though some of the details will differ, of course. So maybe he wanted an outsider's opinion on some of the advice he had received in his own country? Though I have to say that mostly the people who come to see me are interested in setting up their own estate. Making sure that everything is in order before they pass away."

"He does have a wife and kids," said Odelia.

"Maybe he was considering a move to the United States? And bringing his family along with him? In that case, he would have been covered by our laws in regards to inheritance, and if that were so, my advice would have been more apt than the advice of my Abou-Yamen colleagues."

Odelia nodded thoughtfully. "One final question, if I may."

"Of course. Shoot," he said, then grimaced. "That's probably not the right word under the circumstances."

She had taken out her phone and showed pictures of Jonny Carew and Jerry Vale. "Do you recognize these men?"

He studied the pictures for a moment. "Are these …"

"Yes, these are the shooters. Both from last night and yesterday morning."

He shook his head. "Can't say I've ever seen them before."

"We think they were hired by a third party—the person behind this whole thing."

"So what about the people you arrested yesterday? Maybe they're also behind this?"

"They're denying any involvement, either with the murder of the prince, or the shootings. And we haven't been able to find a link with Vale and Carew either, or any phone calls or messages back and forth—not even any suspicious deposits or payments into their bank account. Unless of course they were using a second phone and a separate bank account."

He handed her back her phone. "It's extremely frustrating, as I have a lot of work to get back to. And I can only do so much by working remotely. So the sooner you find the person or persons responsible—or discover the reason why this is all happening, the better for me." He held up his hand. "Not that I want to put undue pressure on you, of course, Odelia."

"That's all right. We're used to working under pressure, my husband and I."

"Is that unusual? A reporter and a cop collaborating?"

She smiled and settled back on the couch. Charlene came in with a tray carrying cups of coffee and cookies and distributed them among the present company, much to the delight of Odelia, who's a real coffee nut. "Yes, it is a little unusual," she agreed. "But it seems to work. My uncle says we make a great team, so he keeps sending us out in the field to catch killers and solve crimes."

"And you do a great job, too," said Charlene, joining the conversation. She turned to the lawyer. "Odelia has the emotional intelligence to make any suspect or witness open up to her in no time, while Chase has that analytical mind to make sense of things and make connections. It doesn't hurt that he looks like a tough guy and can put the fear of God into a suspect."

"He's a real sweetheart, though," Odelia assured the lawyer. "He may look tough but he's actually a teddy bear."

"He is," said Charlene with a smile. "Just like Alec. He may look like this big grumpy bruiser but deep down he's a softie."

"Good to know," said the lawyer as he took a sip from his

coffee. "Well, I wish I could help you more. It's extremely frustrating to me that I'm being targeted and I don't even know why."

"We'll get to the bottom of it," said Odelia. She turned to me and gave me a wink. Which meant she wanted *me* to get to the bottom of it. And since I had absolutely no idea what was going on, I gulped a little.

Maybe Gran should buzz me with that bug spray, I thought. It might make my brain cells proliferate and work twice as hard as they were working now. Maybe then I'd finally have that breakthrough we were all looking for!

CHAPTER 29

Once again, we found ourselves at the General Store, being entertained by Kingman and invited to sample some of the kibble that his owner had put out for any passing cat. The bowl that emptied out the fastest would win flavor of the day, and its supplier would get a nice backfill order from Wilbur. The one that didn't get any love at all would be removed from sale. It was a simple system, and frankly speaking, the only system that was fair: cat food being sampled by actual cats. How much fairer could it get?

There had been a short while when Wilbur had done away with the system, but that had led to a lot of complaints from Hampton Cove's cats. And after being informed by Gran, the shopkeeper had reinstalled the old system. At the time, he had claimed that it was costing him an arm and a leg and that the General Store wasn't as successful as it used to be. But after Odelia had written a nice puff piece on Wilbur and the store, things had turned around. So much so that the man's famous tasters had returned—and a good thing, too, for with all this traipsing across town on our investigations, I got a little peckish from time to time, and to dip into Kingman's bowls was always a welcome thing.

"So what do you think?" asked the large cat as he gave me a critical look. "Tastes just the same, doesn't it?"

"It does," I confirmed. "It *is* the same. Exactly the same."

"And yet it comes in two different bags!" he cried, pointing to the bags in question, located inside the store. We followed him, and he showed us the bags in question. One was called 'Perfect Pet Food For The Discerning Cat,' and the other was called 'Pet Food To Make Your Cat Go Giddy.' Though it could have been something different.

"Two different brands, and yet they're identical," he said. "Now isn't that something?"

"It certainly is," I said. I didn't know what it was, but it was something for sure.

"I like them both," said Dooley. "I honestly don't know what to choose this time, Kingman."

"That's because it's the same kibble, buddy," said the big cat.

"Oh? But then why did you put it in two different bowls?"

Kingman smiled and placed a paw on Dooley's shoulder. "It's a long story, and not one I'm sure you want to hear. Suffice it to say that *I* didn't put that kibble in those bowls. Wilbur did, and since he doesn't know what this stuff tastes like, since he's not a cat, he trusts our judgment. The problem is that we can't convey our opinion, so we do it by emptying one bowl and not touching the other, do you see?"

"Not really," said Dooley with a frown. "You're right that it all sounds very complicated, Kingman. So can you give us the gist?"

"The gist is that we're being hoodwinked, buddy!" said Kingman, throwing up his paws. "And I want you to talk to Odelia and tell her, so she can tell Wilbur not to buy from these people again. Or maybe she can launch an investigation and write about it in that paper of hers. It sure sounds like something people should know."

"I guess," said Dooley, though he still didn't look as if he understood what was going on.

Kingman directed a curious look at Harriet. "You didn't touch the kibble. What's wrong?"

"I don't feel so good," said Harriet, and coughed.

"Gran sprayed her with bug spray," Brutus said. "She wanted her to have kittens, but that didn't work out so well."

"Instead of kittens, she got cooties," said Dooley.

"I feel sick," Harriet confessed. "But at least I didn't lose my voice," she added proudly. "Wanna hear?"

"Well…" said Kingman, giving me an uncertain look. When I shook my head, he plastered a forced smile on his face. "Sure. Why not."

"Pick a song," said Harriet. "Any song."

"Um… how about *I Want to Know What Love Is?*" he suggested.

Harriet smiled, closed her eyes, and launched into a heart-wrenching—and gut-clenching—rendition of the popular ballad. All around us, people stopped to take notice, and the customers inside Wilbur's store all came out to see what was going on. Possibly expecting another drive-by shooting. Instead they all formed a circle around our friend, who sang her little heart out. When she had finished, they all clapped, and she took a curtsy in response.

"Amazing," said one customer. "What a voice."

"It sounded as if someone had stepped on her tail," said another one.

"Is she ill, do you think?" asked a third. "She sounds ill."

"I think she's lost," said a fourth. "She's screaming for her human to come find her."

"Maybe we should call the police," said another one. "Or the pound?"

"Let's... not call the pound," said Wilbur, deciding to step in before someone took Harriet and carted her off to the pound. He picked her up and carried her inside. "Best not to start screaming in front of my store. People take it the wrong way. Think I've been torturing you."

"But I wasn't screaming," said Harriet. "I was singing."

He carried her into the private space at the back of the store, and we all followed, just to make sure she would be all right. When we passed through the string curtain at the end of the store and found ourselves in Wilbur's kitchen, it immediately became clear that Harriet wasn't doing so well. She sneezed up a storm and looked even sicker than before.

"Wilbur said I was screaming, you guys," she said, "but I wasn't. I was singing! A beautiful song!"

"And it certainly was beautiful," I told her soothingly. "It's just that these humans can't understand you, you see."

"And also, they have no taste," Brutus added.

"No taste whatsoever," said Kingman.

"And stay there," said Wilbur as he pointed to the floor where he had placed Harriet. "Unless you want to clear out my store again." He shook his head as he walked away and disappeared through the door.

"He's not very nice to me, is he," said Harriet. Then she turned to Kingman. "How you can stand to be around that man is a mystery to me, Kingman."

"You're a real hero," I told the big cat.

"I know," said Kingman modestly. "But then I guess you can get used to anything." He grinned. "I'm just kidding. Wilbur isn't so bad. He takes some getting used to, that's true, but that can be said about all of us. Even me, the most agreeable cat on the planet."

Harriet sneezed again. "I'm also very agreeable. I have to

be, for it's tough to break into show business. You have to be a real people's cat. At least in the beginning. Once you're a star you can let your inner diva out, but until then, you have to get along with people or they won't give you a chance to shine." She sneezed once more and groaned. "What's wrong with me?"

"Looks like that medicine Vena gave you isn't working so well," I said. I looked over to Kingman. "Maybe we better alert our human. She should take Harriet back to the vet."

"No vet!" said Harriet. "Once a day is quite enough, wouldn't you say? No, I'm fine. Especially since I still have my voice." She sneezed again, really loud this time. "Oh, God. I don't like to be sick," she said. "In fact, I hate it."

We all stood around her, and I have to say I was worried about Harriet. This spray Gran had applied to her clearly didn't work as advertised. First of all, it said that it wasn't harmful for humans and pets, but that obviously wasn't the case. And secondly, it seemed to make pests increase in number instead of get rid of them, so that was a double failure in my book.

"Maybe the spray is making the germs inside you proliferate," I said.

"You think?" asked Harriet, who had collapsed on the floor now and looked too weak to stand on her own four feet.

"Let's call the vet," I said.

"But how?" asked Kingman.

"Leave that to me," I said determinedly. And I hurried off through the string curtain designed to keep flies out, and through the store, weaving my way through the legs of Wilbur's customers and out the door. As I did, suddenly I thought I recognized two of Wilbur's customers. They were… Johnny and Jerry! Only they were wearing disguises. Both had donned wigs and mustaches, but that didn't fool me. Another good reason to tell Odelia she had to hurry over.

I made it to the *Gazette* offices in record time and sped through the door of my human's office, a little out of breath but otherwise still capable of crying out, "It's Harriet, Odelia. She's sick again! And also, Johnny and Jerry are at the General Store!"

Odelia didn't waste time asking a ton of questions. Instead, she grabbed her phone and followed me out. And as she did, she put a call to her husband and also to Vena to meet her at the General Store. Then she picked me up and ran all the way over to the store without delay.

"Vena gave her something," she said. "But clearly it wasn't strong enough."

"Whoever made that bug spray should be in jail," I said.

"That's convenient, because they already are in jail. For the murder of Prince Abdullah."

She slammed into the store and her eyes scanned the crowd until they landed on the figures of Johnny and Jerry. The moment they saw her, they instantly turned around and escaped in the direction of the back of the store, through that same fly curtain and into Wilbur's private space.

"Hey!" said Wilbur. "That's private!"

But the two crooks didn't care. And as we hurried after them, we saw that they had already come and gone.

Harriet, Brutus, Dooley, and Kingman, still on the floor, pointed to the back. "They left that way," said Kingman.

Odelia and I hurried over in that direction and saw that the crooks were trying to clamber over the wall that backed Wilbur's small garden. They weren't having a lot of luck, though, and I saw that Johnny's mustache had fallen off his face and Jerry's wig had fallen off his head.

"Stop right there!" Odelia yelled. "You're both under arrest!"

"Not again!" said Johnny as he gave up trying to climb that wall. His partner in crime was on top of the wall, and had a tough decision to make: to leave his partner behind, or get caught along with him. Finally, he decided that he couldn't leave his buddy in the lurch and jumped back down. Both men raised their hands.

"Hi, Odelia," said Jerry pleasantly. "Nice to see you again. How are things?"

"Things are fine," said Odelia. "Don't move, all right?"

"And how is Grace? Growing into a fine young lady?"

"We met your cats last night," said Johnny. "They got into our van. I dropped them off at the house."

"Yeah, I saw that," she said, not as friendly as the two crooks may have liked. She glanced nervously behind her, eager for the cavalry to arrive.

"We keep meeting like this," said Jerry. "Not that I'm complaining."

"It's fun to catch up with old friends," Johnny pointed out.

"Maybe we could all sit down for dinner one time? You and Marge and your grandma. I would like that."

"Me too," said Johnny. "I would like that very much."

"How is your mom?"

"My mom is fine," said Odelia curtly.

"I like Marge," said Johnny warmly. "She's great."

"I also like Marge," said Jerry. "What a lady."

"What a woman," Johnny concurred. "If I wasn't married, and she wasn't married…" He thought for a moment. "I mean, I'm not married, but if she wasn't married…" He seemed to have lost the thread of his argument. "What would you do if Marge wasn't married, Jer?"

"I would take her out to dinner for sure," said Jerry.

"But *I* would like to take her out to dinner," said Johnny.

"We could both take her out to dinner," Jerry suggested.

"And let the best man win?"

"Something like that. Though of course she would choose me."

"I think she would choose me," said Johnny.

"Obviously she would choose me," said Jerry.

Johnny's bonhomous mood turned. "And I'm telling you she would choose me!"

"No, she would choose me!"

"She would choose neither of you," said Odelia, settling the matter. "Because she's already married, remember?"

"Oh," said Johnny. "I forgot about that."

"Why did you try to shoot Rogelio Hartshorn?" asked Odelia, figuring that now that the men were in such a talkative mood she might as well ask the question.

Johnny shrugged. "Who's Rogelio Hartshorn?"

"The man you tried to shoot yesterday."

"Oh, *that* guy. I didn't even know his name was Rogelio Hartshorn."

"I knew," said Jerry.

"That's because you're in charge of admin, Jer," Johnny reminded him.

"Can I lower my arms now?" asked Jerry. "They're getting tired."

"No, keep them up," said Odelia.

"What was the question again?"

"Why did you try to shoot Mr. Hartshorn?"

"Because it's our job?"

"A well-paying job, too," said Johnny.

"Yeah, a *very* well-paying job," said Jerry.

"Only we haven't been paid yet, have we, Jer?"

"That's because he's still alive, you doofus. And if you hadn't missed—twice!—we would have been paid by now."

"Who's paying you to shoot him?" asked Odelia.

Johnny shrugged and turned to his friend. "Who hired us, Jer?"

"No idea," said Jerry. "Can I lower my arms now?"

"No!" said Odelia. "What do you mean you don't know who's paying you?"

"I never met the guy, did I?" said Jerry in an apologetic tone.

"That's the internet for you, Odelia," Johnny explained. "It's all done online and you don't get to meet people anymore. I liked it much more in the old days when you got to know your clients. Sit down with them, you know. This internet business…" He made a face. "Very impersonal, if you know what I mean. Takes a lot of the fun out of the whole thing."

"So, someone contacted you online and hired you to kill Rogelio?" asked Odelia.

"Yeah, something like that," said Jerry. "Can I lower my arms now?"

"No! Who contacted you?"

"What was the guy's name, Jer?" asked Johnny.

"No idea. Something with a V and an M, I think."

"Vladimir?" Johnny suggested.

"I'd have to check my phone. Can I—"

"No!"

Just then, Chase and some of his officers came hurrying into the backyard and quickly and efficiently placed both men under arrest. "Thanks, detective," said Jerry as he cast a dirty look at Odelia. "And can you tell your wife that she shouldn't yell at us like that?"

"Especially after we invited her to dinner?" Johnny added.

"It's not very nice," said Jerry.

"Not very sociable. Especially considering we've known each other for years."

"And her mother is such a good friend of ours," Jerry added.

"I still think she would marry *me*," said Jerry as both men were being led away.

"And I'm telling you she would marry *me*," said Johnny.

"She likes me best."

"No, she likes *me* best!"

Odelia rubbed the side of her face. "Oh, boy," she said, and that summed things up quite nicely, I thought.

CHAPTER 30

As it turned out, Johnny and Jerry had entered the modern era and had been hired over Telegram to carry out their nefarious designs on Rogelio. Since they had lost the man last night and would only get paid once they had effectively carried out their assignment, they decided that the General Store was as good a place as any to gather information about the possible whereabouts of the estate lawyer. When asked by Chase why the lawyer had to die, they had absolutely no idea. Even though all of the communication was available on Jerry's phone, there wasn't a lot that could be gleaned as the person doing the hiring had most likely used a false name and their credentials were impossible to determine. In other words: another dead end.

When asked if they were also involved in the murder of Prince Abdullah, they declined all knowledge of that murder and claimed they hadn't even been anywhere near the hotel when it happened. In other words: baffling—very baffling!

Odelia and Chase decided to take their troubles to Cup o' Mika, a nearby coffee shop, and discuss the case, with Dooley and me seated underneath their table. Harriet and

Brutus were still at Vena's, where the vet wanted to keep Harriet under observation and make sure she was all right. She had extracted some blood from our unfortunate friend and, depending on the results, would decide how to proceed. It was, in other words, a troubling time for all of us.

"I hope Harriet will be all right," said Odelia as she thanked the waitress for the slice of blueberry pie and the cup of coffee and took a sip from the invigorating brew.

"She'll be fine," said Chase. "Though you may want to keep an eye on your grandmother. If she's poisoning the cats now, there's no telling what she will do next. She might poison *us*."

"I don't think she would go that far," said Odelia, though she clearly wasn't fully convinced herself that this was the case.

"As long as Harriet can keep singing, I think she will be fine," said Dooley.

"The singing is all right," I said. "But it's the nausea that worries me. Clearly, she has been poisoned with the horrible stuff that came out of that can."

"Bug spray," said Dooley, "probably shouldn't be used on cats."

"Tell that to Gran," I said. I shivered. It's one thing for crooks like Johnny and Jerry to lock us up and threaten our lives, but another for our own human to make us sick with poisoning symptoms. Gran clearly had crossed a line that should never have been crossed.

"Okay, so to recap," said Chase. "We've got Vale and Carew confessing that they tried to kill Rogelio, but they don't know why and they don't know who hired them, except that his name is Vladimir, which is obviously a fake name, so that's effectively another dead end. And then there's the murder of Prince Abdullah, which they claim they weren't involved in."

"Do you believe them?" asked Odelia.

"As a matter of fact, I do. Vale and Carew may be a lot of things, but they're pretty straightforward when it comes to their criminal activities. They even seem to take a certain pride in what they do. So if they say they weren't involved, I believe them. Also, it's not their style. They're pretty crude, not to mention clumsy operators. The murder of Prince Abdullah was planned and executed with precision, the murder weapon planted on those bug spray salespeople."

"So now you believe that they are innocent as well, do you?"

"Yeah, I guess so. I really don't see the motive, do you? Also, they don't have any priors and they don't exactly strike me as guns for hire."

"No, I guess not," said Odelia as she bit into the blueberry pie and closed her eyes with relish. "Yum. This stuff is pretty good. You should try some."

Dooley and I watched with a sad eye. Sugar is strictly off-limits for us, and to watch our human enjoy it so much made my stomach rumble a little in anticipation of something hearty and filling. "Too bad these tea rooms never seem to have anything edible for the likes of us," I complained.

"Maybe if you ask them?" Dooley suggested. "Or we could always return to the General Store and have some more of Kingman's kibble?"

"No thank you very much," I said. "That stuff is pretty much inedible."

"It was tasteless. And also odorless and didn't have a lot of texture either."

"I didn't like it," I said. "Neither of the two samples."

"I wonder who would sell the same kibble twice, and put it in different packaging and sell it at different prices?" Dooley asked.

It was another mystery we needed to get to the bottom of,

but it didn't seem all that urgent compared to the mystery of the dead prince and the attempted murder of Rogelio Hartshorn.

A familiar person came trotting up and joined us at our table. It was Gran, and she looked extremely subdued and even contrite. "How is Harriet?" she asked.

"Not well," said Odelia firmly. "She was poisoned."

"I'm so sorry," said Gran, wringing her hands. "If only I had known."

"A sane person would never spray their cats with bug spray," Odelia pointed out. "But then of course that is too much to expect from you, isn't it, Gran?"

Gran bowed her head. "I'm so, so, so very sorry. How can I make it up to you?"

"It's not me you should be apologizing to but Harriet. What were you thinking?"

"I was thinking that I had a winner on my hands," said Gran. "When I saw that the bug spray caused the bugs to increase in number instead of croak, I figured I had something that was going to make us all rich beyond belief. But instead, I got this dreadful poison."

"I wonder what kind of person sells bug spray that doesn't kill bugs but poisons pets instead," said Chase. "I mean, has this stuff even been approved by the FDA?"

"It certainly raises all kinds of questions about the ethics of Carlos Perks and Mindy Horsefield," said Odelia. She shared a look with her husband. "Though I don't see what connection there could possibly be with the murder of Prince Abdullah."

"No, I don't see it either," Chase confessed.

Gran got up. "I'll go and pay a visit to Vena and see how Harriet is doing." Before she left, she dug into her purse and handed both me and Dooley a piece of sausage. She smiled. "To make amends," she explained. And then she shuffled off, looking extremely unhappy. Even though she was fully to blame for what had happened, at least she understood that she had made a terrible mistake and was repentant. The same couldn't be said about Johnny and Jerry, who seemed to consider the attempted murder of Rogelio a simple business transaction and regretted not having been able to get their guy, since that meant they wouldn't get paid.

I sniffed at the piece of sausage. It smelled fine. I dug my teeth into it. It was delish.

"Do you think whoever hired Vale and Carew will go a different route and try to hire a different hitman?" asked Odelia.

"It's possible," said Chase. "And as long as we don't know who the client is, Rogelio won't be safe."

I glanced across the street and thought I saw a familiar face in the crowd. It was a man and he was studying us intently. Wearing sunglasses and a ball cap to cover the upper portion of his face. It was hard to be sure, but I could have sworn I had seen this man before.

"Dooley," I said, drawing my friend's attention to the man. "Isn't that the hotel manager who locked us up in his office?"

"Yeah, that's him," said Dooley. "He's watching us, Max."

"He sure is."

"Do you think he's still sore that we asked Norm to help us escape from his office?"

"He doesn't know that we did that," I said. "Most people think that cats are dumb creatures. No, I'm sure it's not us he's watching but Chase and Odelia."

"But why? Maybe he wants to rent them a room for the night?"

"I doubt it. Hotel managers have different ways of finding potential clients than stalking them across town. No, whatever interest he has in Odelia and Chase must be connected to…" I swallowed down a piece of sausage. And then suddenly a lightbulb seemed to go off in my head. I stared at my friend. "Dooley!" I said.

"Max?"

"I think I've got it! I really think I've got it!"

"Good job, Max," said Dooley warmly. "What have you got?"

"The thing—the whole thing!"

He gave me a look of confusion. "What thing would that be, Max?"

I knew I wasn't making a lot of sense, but then that's par for the course when you suddenly get these brainwaves. At first, they're jumbled and muddled. But with a little effort from that old noggin of mine, I knew I'd get there. And so I tapped Odelia on the knee and told her all about my lightbulb moment. She seemed strangely intrigued and whispered to her husband, "Don't look now, but the manager of the Star Hotel is watching us from across the street."

Chase knew better than to turn to stare at the guy, but he casually stretched out and glanced in the direction indicated before murmuring, "Now what does he want from us?"

And that's when Odelia told him all about my big idea. Chase smiled. "I'll call the embassy immediately and set up a meeting." He patted my head. "If what you're saying is true, Max, I will personally go out and buy the best treat that you've ever had. How does that sound?"

That sounded pretty great, especially after all the excitement of the past couple of days. That's the advantage of having a cat detective in your employ: you don't have to pay him an arm and a leg. All he needs is the occasional caress, pat on the head, and some decent grub.

CHAPTER 31

Harriet was feeling a lot better already. She had been plagued by that sudden feeling of nausea, but Vena had given her something for her stomach and the nausea had gradually abated. Now she was actually feeling hungry. Vena had kept her at the office to keep an eye on her, and Brutus, being the loyal boyfriend that he was, had stayed with her for the duration.

"Pookie?" she said from her vantage point on the couch that Vena had placed in her office.

"Yes, buttercup?" said Brutus, immediately raising his head in response.

"Could you fetch me something to eat? It's just that I'm suddenly very hungry."

The smile he displayed was something to behold. "Oh, but that's great news! So the nausea?"

"Gone," she said proudly. "I seem to have kicked the disease or bug or whatever it was, and I'm feeling right as rain again."

"I guess it's time to go home then," said Brutus as he

stretched and gracefully jumped down from the couch. "Vena is nice and all, but there's no place like home."

"I have to say the woman has grown on me," said Harriet. "I always thought she was our worst enemy, always eager to torture us any way she could, but maybe that was a little harsh."

"Yeah, maybe she's not so bad," Brutus agreed. "Though I still wouldn't like to pay her a visit more than is strictly necessary."

"No, I think it's generally a good practice to see your vet as little as possible. Better for your health."

She glanced around and saw that Vena had decorated her office and made it a very cozy little place. There were posters on the walls of cats of every possible persuasion, indicating that at heart Vena was a cat person, which probably wouldn't sit well with the dog owners that paid her for her services. Though she also spotted a nice portrait of a horse, which told her that the vet also had a soft spot for that species.

On Vena's desk, there was a large plastic Garfield, and on a bulletin board behind the desk, several kids' drawings. "I didn't know Vena had kids," she said. "Did you know, precious?"

"No, I didn't. But then we don't know a lot about the woman, do we?"

"No, we don't," Harriet admitted. She suddenly realized that in all those years of picturing Vena as a monster, they had never stopped to think that she was also a human being and possibly had a husband and a family.

She now saw that the door of Vena's office was ajar and joined her boyfriend on the floor. "Let's go exploring," she suggested. With the nausea subsiding, her sense of adventure had returned.

"Exploring where?" asked Brutus.

"I want to know what makes this woman tick," she said.

"Her heart, I guess," said Brutus, who always did have to take things literally, not a poetic bone in his body.

"No, I mean, what kind of person is she? Behind the mask, I mean."

"I didn't know Vena wore a mask," said Brutus, causing Harriet to execute the perfect eye roll.

"Let's just go and take a look," she said. "I want to know what kind of person we're dealing with here." And she felt she had a right to know, since Vena was more or less the person dealing with life and death of pets in Hampton Cove.

They slipped through the door and found themselves in a well-lit corridor that led to a large room. When they arrived, she saw that it was a living room, and as brightly and cozily decorated as the vet's office. On the couch, two kids were playing a video game, and at the breakfast nook, Vena was pouring herself a cup of coffee while glancing out of the window and into the backyard, which looked like a haven of verdant green and quite inviting, Harriet had to say. In an armchair, an elderly man sat reading a newspaper, and Harriet was surprised that people still read the paper on paper, like in the olden days. At her own home, everyone read on their phones or on tablets these days. Of Vena's husband, if she had a husband, there was not a single trace. Though, of course, the elderly man with the paper could be the husband, but she didn't think so. Vena wasn't that old. Unless she favored older men, of course. A lot older.

"Look there, kit kat," she said, and pointed to a gerbil sitting in a cage in a corner of the room. "She has pets."

"Just the one pet," said Brutus. "And I wouldn't call a gerbil a pet, would you?"

"I would," she said. "Any animal can be a pet." They walked up to the gerbil and she decided to engage the creature in conversation, curious what it would have to say about Vena.

"Hi there," she said. "My name is Harriet and this is Brutus. We're Vena's patients."

"Hi," said the gerbil, a little shyly. "My name is Jevon, and I'm not a patient."

"No, I didn't think you were," she said with a laugh. "So what I wanted to ask you: what is Vena like? I mean, is she a good person, you think? A good pet parent?"

"Oh, I can't complain," said the gerbil. "She treats me well enough, I guess. Feeds me on a regular basis, plays with me from time to time, and even gives me a treat on occasion."

He didn't sound very excited, she thought.

"But…" she prompted, feeling there was a 'but' coming.

"Well, I would like to be let out of this cage more often, you know. Be like you guys: allowed to walk around and go wherever I like."

"You're always locked up in this cage?"

"They do take me out from time to time, but then they always put me back. And I don't like it," he said, his face sagging a little as he darted a glance at his human. "She says I can't be trusted outside of my cage. Says there's a flight risk, whatever that means."

"It means she's afraid you will escape," Harriet explained.

"Have you tried to escape, Jevon?" asked Brutus.

"Of course I have tried to escape," said the gerbil. "Wouldn't you try to escape when they keep you locked up twenty-four-seven? I've tried to escape so many times I've lost count, but every time they catch me, and now they practically never let me out of here."

"Maybe if you stopped trying to escape, they would let you out more often," Harriet suggested.

"Fat chance," he scoffed. "I have a feeling that I'll be in this cage until the day I die. And let me tell you that's not a fun prospect. Like being a prisoner, you know. Sentenced to life in jail."

It certainly was not a nice prospect, Harriet agreed, and wondered if they couldn't do something to make life more fun and pleasant for the gerbil. "Okay, so the thing is that Brutus and I can talk to our humans," she said. "So what if we told them about you and they talked to Vena and asked her to let you out more often? How would you feel about that?"

"But only if you promised not to try to escape anymore," said Brutus. "You'd have to be good, you know."

"Oh, I'd be good," said the gerbil. "If I can just potter around in here, and also in the backyard, I wouldn't have to escape, would I?"

It was one of those things, Harriet saw. A vicious circle. They kept Jevon locked up because he tried to escape, and he tried to escape because they kept him locked up. And she now saw that it was up to her to break the cycle. And so she gave the gerbil a reassuring smile. "We'll talk to Odelia, and she'll talk to Vena, and you'll be out of here in a jiffy. Just you wait and see."

"Are you sure?" asked the gerbil hopefully. "Because I've been promised stuff before, and it never happened."

"Who has promised you stuff?" asked Brutus.

The gerbil pointed to the kids on the sofa. "Them. They said they would always love me and play with me, but look at them. All they do is play their video games and they never even look at me anymore. It used to be different. When I first came to live with them, they were always fussing over me and couldn't get enough of me. But that didn't last very long, did it?"

"That's kids for you," said Brutus. "You were just their latest toy until they replaced you with a different one."

"It's sad," said the gerbil. "Very sad."

Harriet wondered if they couldn't adopt the gerbil. She was sure that Grace would love to play with him. But then they couldn't really do that. Vena wouldn't like it.

"We'll just have to educate those kids," she said. "And make them understand that you're not a toy but a member of the family. That they can't just discard you like yesterday's paper."

"We'll talk to Odelia," said Brutus. "And we'll make sure that your life will vastly improve, little buddy."

The gerbil gave them a tentative smile. "Who are you guys? Santa's little helpers?"

Harriet grinned, and a warm glow spread through her chest. "That's exactly who we are. We're Santa's little helpers, and we go around making the lives of pets like us better."

"I hope Vena will listen to you," said Jevon. "Cause I would like my life to improve, you know. It's been pretty rotten so far."

"I know," said Harriet, and wondered if Vena knew that her gerbil was unhappy. It wasn't enough to clean out his cage on a regular basis and provide food and water. Pets needed more than that. They also needed to be cherished and to feel like they were members of the family and paid attention to. In other words: they needed what every person in the world needs.

They said their goodbyes to the gerbil and snuck back out of the living room of the vet and into her office, awaiting Odelia's return so they could go home again. Harriet felt a renewed sense of purpose. "We're Santa's helpers now, lemon drop," she said. "We're on a mission to make the world a better place for pets."

"I like that," said Brutus. "I like being Santa's little helper."

They both looked up when Vena stuck her head around the corner to look in on them. When she saw they were still where she had left them, she seemed satisfied because she smiled and retracted her head again.

Yep, Vena was a human being just like any other, Harriet thought. So not a vicious monster after all. Who knew!

CHAPTER 32

Scarlett met Vesta on the corner of Norfolk Street and saw that her friend wasn't in the best of moods. In fact, she looked downright terrible. "Honey, what's wrong?" she asked.

"I did the most horrible thing, Scarlett," said Vesta. "I poisoned Harriet. She's at the vet right now, and things are not looking good."

"Oh, but that's terrible," she said with feeling. Even though she had only recently adopted Clarice, she had already become very attached to the sweetheart and couldn't imagine life without her. "When you say things are not looking good, you mean…"

Vesta shook her head. "I don't know. Odelia wouldn't say. Just that she's suffering from an acute case of nausea, and she had to take her to Vena twice already. She's there right now, with Vena wanting to keep her under observation." She buried her face in her hands. "Oh, honey, if anything happens to Harriet, I won't be able to forgive myself."

"It's the bug spray, isn't it? We shouldn't have trusted our own judgment and should have had it tested before applying it to Harriet."

"I should have tested it on a rat, just like you suggested," said Vesta. "Though poor rat, you know." A hard look came into her eyes. "It's those bug spray salespeople. They promised that their product isn't harmful to humans or pets, but clearly they were lying."

"They're still in prison, aren't they?"

"I'm not sure," said Vesta. "I would like a word with them, though. After this mess they made with their bug spray, they've got a lot of explaining to do."

"Let's hope Vena can work a miracle," she said. If anyone could save Harriet, it was Vena Aleman, the most accomplished vet in all of Hampton Cove, with plenty of experience under her belt. And as they stood chatting, suddenly she noticed something quite peculiar. "That guy over there—he's acting suspiciously, wouldn't you say?" She was pointing at Garland McNerlin, the manager of the Star Hotel, who stood across the street from the coffee shop where Vesta's granddaughter sat enjoying a drink with her husband Chase. Clearly, he was watching them and trying to remain inconspicuous about it.

"You're absolutely right," said Vesta with a frown. "What is he up to?"

They'd seen Garland often enough at the Star, their favorite place to have a drink in the morning. He was always friendly and polite to a T, so this type of behavior was quite out of character. Also, instead of donning his usual suit, he had opted for jeans and a T-shirt, which made him look odd. But then she wasn't used to seeing him out of his usual attire —or even outside his usual surroundings. Odelia and Chase got up, paid for their beverages, then started in the direction of the police station. Without delay, the manager started following them!

"Well, I'll be damned," said Vesta. "Let's see what he's up to." And so they followed the guy, to make sure he didn't get Odelia and Chase into any trouble.

"Maybe they forgot to pay their bill?" Scarlett suggested.

"No hotel manager would follow his guests if they haven't paid their bills," Vesta said, and that sure made sense to Scarlett. Imagine if a hotel manager had to start stalking all of his welching customers. There simply weren't enough hours in the day.

Odelia and Chase got into Chase's squad car. The manager seemed to hesitate, but only for a moment. Then he hurried to a cab parked on the corner of the street and got in.

"We're going to lose him, Vesta," said Scarlett. "He's getting away!"

"No, he isn't," said Vesta determinedly. And so she stepped out into the street and started waving her arms until the driver of the next car stopped. With screeching tires, he pulled up right in front of her, with only millimeters to spare. The guy stuck his head out of his car. "Hey lady, are you nuts!" he yelled.

But Vesta didn't waste time arguing. Instead, she yanked open the passenger side door and stepped into the car. "Get in!" she told Scarlett. And so Scarlett did as she was told.

"Hey! What do you think you're doing!" the guy cried.

"I'm Vesta Muffin, and I'm the leader of the neighborhood watch," said Vesta, producing the neighborhood watch badge she had especially printed for this type of occasion. "And I want you to follow that cab!"

"I ain't doing no such thing!" the guy said, folding his arms across a very hairy chest.

"Follow that cab, or I'll have to arrest you for obstruction of a neighborhood watch investigation!" she said.

"There's no such thing as a neighborhood watch investigation!"

"Oh, yes, there is. We work with the police. So either you do as you're told, or you will face the consequences." She leaned in, her breath hot on the man's face. "I'm not kidding, bozo!"

"All right, all right," said the guy, and put his car in gear again, then stomped on the accelerator and went in pursuit of the cab that carried the hotel manager. "What's this all about?" asked the man.

"I'm not sure," she said. "But whatever it is, it's not good."

"A man is following Vesta's granddaughter and her husband," Scarlett explained, feeling that they owed their driver at least some explanation.

"Scarlett! That's on a need-to-know basis!"

"I'm driving, so I need to know," the man said, and Scarlett thought he made a good point.

"Okay, so the hotel manager of the Star Hotel is in that cab," she said. "And he's acting very suspiciously. So we want to see what he's up to."

"Gotcha," said the guy, and seemed to warm to his task. "So you're the neighborhood watch, huh?" he said, cutting a glance in his rear-view mirror and flashing a grin at Scarlett. "Must be a pretty exciting job." He was hairy all over, she saw. Apart from the dark curly hair that peeped from his shirt, his face was also covered with the stuff, as well as his brawny arms.

"Oh, it is," she assured him, giving him one of her trademark killer smiles in return. She adjusted her décolletage, which never failed to have a powerful effect on any member of the male sex. "Extremely exciting."

"So do you do this sort of thing often?"

"All the time," she assured him.

"Cool," he said, and stomped on the gas so he was right up on the cab's tail.

"Keep your distance," Vesta advised him. "We don't want him to rumble us."

"Hey, you're the professional, lady," said the guy as he eased up a little and allowed some distance between them and the cab.

"We were so lucky that we got you," said Scarlett, continuing to lay it on thick. It didn't hurt to make the man feel appreciated, she thought. "Our knight in shining armor."

The guy grew a couple of inches in size and grinned. "Cometh the hour, cometh the man."

"That sounds pretty neat," she said. "You probably came up with that all by yourself."

"I *did* come up with that myself! Just now, in fact. I'm very creative that way."

"I'll bet you are…"

"Sean," said the guy. "Sean Odea."

"I'm Scarlett," she said.

"Pleased to meet you, Scarlett."

"The pleasure is all mine, Sean."

The man practically vibrated from sheer excitement.

The cab sped on after Chase's car, and they sped on after the cab. She now wondered if they shouldn't have called for backup in some way. Then again, they were the neighborhood watch, so they shouldn't need backup. Also, the man they were chasing was a hotel manager, not some murderous maniac, so they should be fine. She still couldn't understand why Garland would be following Odelia and Chase around, but hopefully all would be clear soon. Probably it was something entirely innocuous, but it was obvious that Vesta felt she had some making up to do after poisoning Harriet, so Scarlett was determined to let her.

Odelia was pretty upset with her grandmother right now, and anything Vesta could do to atone might get her back in Odelia's good graces—if Harriet lived to tell the tale. If not…

It was doubtful Odelia would ever forgive her.

CHAPTER 33

Rogelio was pacing the living room of the house where he was holed up. It was a nice place, as houses go, but it wasn't home, and so he felt constrained. He had a ton of work and clients he needed to get back to, and he didn't like that he couldn't go to the office to deal with the stack of files on his desk. He had already told his PA that he would be out of the office for a couple of days and that he would work from home, but that cop had told him that he should be careful with that. Whoever was gunning for him might be able to trace his whereabouts by tracking his phone or his laptop, and so he probably should keep them turned off for now.

If only he had never gotten involved with the prince. The man was dead, and still he was haunting him from across the grave, causing untold trouble. If only he knew what it was all about. But since he didn't have the faintest idea, he felt this could take forever, with the wheels of justice moving at a snail's pace as they always did. Progress in the case, if there was any, took its time to trickle through to him—the victim in all of this. It just wasn't fair, he felt.

He allowed himself to drop down onto the couch and gazed idly out of the window and into the backyard, which was nice to look at, but also exceedingly boring. He was a very busy and sociable creature and he missed his regular haunts: the restaurants where he liked to take his clients, the art exhibitions where he took in some culture, the parties he liked to frequent... Life was buzzing at the moment and he was missing all of it. Already he had missed his best friend's daughter's bat mitzvah, and plenty of other unmissable social occasions. And when he told that detective, the guy simply placed a heavy hand on his shoulder, looked him deeply into his eyes, and asked him if he wanted to live. If yes, he should just do as he was told.

Easy for him to say!

The three dogs belonging to his hostess tripped up to him and regarded him curiously. They were miniature poodles, and as he understood, actually belonged to her ex-sister-in-law, who was in prison for some offense she had committed. Not that he was even remotely interested, so he hadn't really listened when the mayor told him about the woman's misadventures.

He should feel honored that the mayor of Hampton Cove herself and her police chief husband were providing him with safe harbor, but the inconvenience still irked him terribly, like an itch he couldn't scratch.

The doggies barked happily and seemed eager for him to play with them, so he ignored Chief Lip's instructions and opened the sliding glass door to let them out into the backyard and followed them there. It wouldn't hurt to throw the ball around a little, would it? Whoever was after him wouldn't ever find him here, would they? And so for the next twenty minutes, he enjoyed himself by throwing the ball and watching those three doggies chase after it like crazy. Oh, they loved it. They loved it so much! Even he had to admit he enjoyed it tremendously.

He'd never thought about getting a dog, figuring dogs were a nuisance and a constraint on his social life, but he was starting to see the appeal. They really were the perfect companions!

And as he watched them chase the ball into the shrubberies, suddenly he saw that two cats had appeared. They were a big black bruiser of a fellow and a gorgeous white Persian.

"Now where did you guys come from all of a sudden?" he asked.

They seemed to be conversing with the dogs, though of course that was entirely impossible. Still, the dogs seemed curiously fascinated by the two cats, and for a moment they sniffed at one another, as animals do, and the ball lost its big attraction. He sank down on a deck chair and closed his eyes. It was at that moment that a shadow fell over him, and when he opened his eyes again, he saw that a man was standing not ten feet away, pointing a gun right at him!

Immediately, he jerked up and out of that deck chair.

"Hey, what do you think you're doing!" he cried.

"You're not an easy man to find, buddy," said the guy. "So this is the rock you've selected to crawl underneath, huh?" He glanced around. "Not too shabby, as rocks go, I have to say."

And then all of a sudden a lot of things seemed to be happening all at once. The three dogs attached themselves to the man's calves, digging their teeth into them. The two cats hurled themselves at the guy, digging their claws into his arm and dragging down his gun hand. Two more cats, a small fluffy one and a big red one, also joined the fray and jumped on top of the man's head! And then out of nowhere, that big cop came charging onto the scene, and knocked into the killer, flattening him on the lawn. To top it off, two old ladies popped up out of the blue and sat on the guy's head, screaming something about a citizen's arrest for the neighborhood watch! And then another guy, that he had never seen before, picked up the gun that had gone skittering across the deck, before being told to drop it by Odelia Kingsley.

The guy immediately complied and held up his hands to prove his innocence.

Rogelio's jaw had dropped from the moment he had laid eyes on his attacker, and he hadn't stopped gaping as the whole amazing sequence of events played out. The upshot was that the wannabe assassin was being placed under arrest and outfitted with a pair of shiny handcuffs as supplied by Detective Kingsley.

"Wha-wha-what just happened?" he stammered.

"The man who was hired to kill you has been arrested," Odelia explained.

"But... I don't understand. Who is he? Why did he want to kill me? And how did he know where I was?" So many questions, but Odelia seemed reluctant to give him any answers.

Instead, she said, "Better stay here for the time being. We've asked for a patrol car to arrive shortly. Two officers will keep an eye on you." And then she was off, to interview the killer.

The four cats and three dogs, meanwhile, sat gazing up at him expectantly, and he understood that they'd probably saved his life. So he patted them on the head, one after the other, then entered the house to look for some nice grub in the fridge that he could give them. They had certainly earned it. And as he dug around in the fridge, suddenly he started shaking all over, and his knees buckled and he started sobbing like a little baby.

Looked like the scariness of the moment was finally catching up with him.

He sat with his back against the fridge, and the three dogs and four cats actually gathered around, and gave him licks on his hands and nudges with their heads.

This is when he understood that pets are the greatest creatures alive, and he vowed to become a pet parent himself as soon as this terrible ordeal was over.

The two old ladies walked in, and also the strange man, and helped him to his feet. He now recognized one of the old ladies as Vesta Muffin, and the other woman as her friend Scarlett Canyon, and the man said he was their driver and he was thinking about joining the neighborhood watch.

It was all a little much for Rogelio, and as they escorted him to the couch and told him to take a seat, Mrs. Canyon started bombarding him with questions about her will and testament, Mrs. Muffin asked him what he knew about bug spray, and the man told him that he normally didn't believe in picking up hitchhikers but that Vesta hadn't taken no for an answer, and that he didn't regret a single moment since he felt he was playing a part in an action movie.

He told the guy he felt much the same way, told Mrs. Muffin that he didn't know the first thing about bug spray, and told Mrs. Canyon that she should make an appointment with his personal assistant and he'd see what he could do. And then he rolled into a ball and hoped that when he woke up again the world would be a better place, without people trying to shoot him!

CHAPTER 34

Huey, Louie, and Dewey were proud that they had been the first to take down their guest's attacker. And it was true: they had been the first to spring to Rogelio's assistance when he was staring into the barrel of a loaded gun. Harriet and Brutus were second, since apparently they had been in search of pets that needed the assistance of 'Santa's Helpers' as they now called themselves. I was glad to see that Harriet was feeling better and that she hadn't lost her spunk.

After I had told Odelia what I thought was going on, Chase made a couple of phone calls and confirmed that my theory was as good as any other, and so they had decided to test it out in the real world by providing a trail of breadcrumbs for the hotel manager staking us out from across the street. He had immediately taken the bait and followed us to the home of Uncle Alec and Charlene, where he had proceeded to threaten the poor lawyer with violence before being taken down by a combined task force consisting of one detective, one civilian consultant, four cats, three dogs, and two members of the neighborhood watch and their driver. In other words: an overwhelming enemy force that the hotel manager couldn't possibly compete with.

The man had been led away and would have to pay for his crimes. Meanwhile, the lawyer had suffered a sort of breakdown, which was understandable. And since we didn't want to leave him all by himself, we decided to keep him company for now. Gran and Scarlett felt the same way, and took it upon themselves to act as the man's guardian angels until backup arrived. The threat might have been lifted, but that didn't mean he was out of trouble just yet. Their driver had left, but not before repeating how happy he was to have made all of our acquaintance. He seemed grateful for the adventure of a lifetime, as he called it.

"I should never have spritzed you with that bug spray," Gran told Harriet as she stroked her affectionately. "Will you ever be able to forgive me, honey?"

"Of course, Gran," said Harriet. "Though maybe next time when you want a guinea pig, you should find a different one. I didn't enjoy the experience."

"Though we wouldn't have minded having kids, would we, sparky star?" asked Brutus, happy now that he wouldn't have kids after all.

"I'm not sure I want kids, snuggle bug," said Harriet. "It's a lot of work, isn't it, taking care of kids? And such a responsibility. I mean, just look at Chase and Odelia and how much work they have with just the one kid. Imagine the same thing but multiplied by five or six or seven."

"I guess you're right," said Brutus, well pleased. He gave me a wink.

"He looks exhausted," said Scarlett as she cast a worried glance at the estate lawyer.

"Attempts have been made on the man's life no less than

three times in a row," said Gran. "How would you feel if people were trying to kill you all the time?"

"I guess it's not a pleasant experience," said Scarlett. "Though he's safe now, isn't he?"

"I'm not sure," said Gran, giving me a questioning look.

"He's safe for now," I said. "But the people who paid that hotel manager and also Johnny and Jerry to get rid of him are still out there, and they might try again."

"You know, this bug spray might not have worked on Harriet," said Dooley, "but it worked on the bugs in our backyard, didn't it? So maybe it only works on bugs? It *is* called a bug spray, after all, not a pet spray."

"I like your thinking, Dooley," said Gran. "But I'm not going to give it any more tries. I'm glad that Harriet is fine, and I'm not going to take any chances from now on."

Just then, a familiar-looking fly came buzzing into the house, took one look around, and settled on the wall next to me. "I've been talking to Norma," he said. "And you'll be happy to know that everything is fine between us. Marriage saved and soon I'm going to be a dad!"

"Oh, Norm, you finally took the plunge!" said Harriet.

"That's great news, Norm," said Brutus. "Congratulations."

"Was it the bug spray that did it, you think?" asked Dooley. "Did Gran zap you with that bug spray and now Norma is pregnant?"

"Bug spray had nothing to do with it, buddy," said Norm. He pounded his little chest. "It's all down to me."

"Congratulations, Norm," I said, well pleased with this good news. "That's great to hear. And I know you'll be a great father to those kids."

"Is it a boy or a girl?" asked Dooley.

Norm grinned, or at least I thought he did. It's hard to

read a fly as their facial features are a little different from ours. "I guess there will be boys and girls both," he said.

"Oh, you mean you're having twins?" asked Dooley.

"A fly lays over a hundred eggs, Dooley," I said. "So there will be plenty of boys and girls."

He stared at me. "A hundred kids! But how are you going to feed all of them, Norm?"

"Norma found a great stash of food," said Norm, and he seemed to have reconciled himself pretty well with his new role as dad. But then it's different for flies, as their young leave the nest pretty early on and don't stick around like human children do. They sometimes linger on until they're well into their twenties or even their thirties and forties, which seems like a terrible nuisance for their poor parents. Then again, I did hope that Grace would stick around for a long time to come, as I quite enjoyed having her around.

Charlene and Uncle Alec's guest had awakened from his slumber, for he smacked his lips and opened his eyes to look around. When he saw three dogs, four cats, two old ladies, and a fly looking back at him, he blinked and shot up. "I must have fallen asleep," he said.

"That's all right," said Gran, patting him on the arm. "You sleep as much as you like. You've been through a big ordeal, so you need to sleep it off. If you want, I could make you a cup of tea?"

"Coffee," he said immediately. "I mean, if it's not too much trouble."

"Absolutely not," she said, and swiftly got to her feet. "It's my son and daughter-in-law's place, you see," she said. "So I know my way around here pretty well." She started opening kitchen cupboards left and right, proving that she didn't know her way around there any more than we did. It is true that Charlene's place is not a house that we often frequent, though now that she had taken three miniature poodles under wing, that might change. Even though at first we hadn't made a great impression on the doggies, we now got along well. Their human was in prison, serving a sentence for stealing chickens and swindling people out of money, and so Huey, Dewey, and Louie had found a momentary home with Charlene, and they seemed to like it a great deal, too. Even Uncle Alec had taken to them in a big way. I'd always suspected him of being a dog person, and now we had proof that he was, in fact, big on dogs.

"What's going to happen to that poor man, Max?" asked Dewey.

"Yes, are they going to keep shooting at him?" asked Huey.

"He doesn't deserve it," said Louie. "He's very nice."

"He likes to play with us," said Dewey. "And we like humans who play with us."

"We sure do," said Louie. "So we wouldn't like him to get shot, Max."

"I don't think *he* would like to get shot," I said.

"Can you make sure he doesn't get shot?" asked Huey.

Three pairs of dog eyes stared at me intently and pleadingly, and finally, I sighed. "Okay, fine. I'll do whatever I can to make sure he doesn't get shot at again. But I can't make any promises, you hear. Basically it's out of my paws."

"In whose paws is it, then?" asked Dewey.

"This is a matter that can only be handled at the highest level of diplomacy," I said.

"The highest level?" asked Louie. "What's the highest level? The ambassador?"

"Higher," I said.

"The Secretary of State?"

"Higher."

They exchanged a look of surprise. "You mean... the President?"

I nodded sagely. "Only the President can exert the kind of pressure that is needed to make sure that Rogelio survives this ordeal."

"Gosh," said Huey, and that summed things up pretty well.

CHAPTER 35

It was a strange scene that played out in the Oval Office of the White House that day. The President sat on the couch, listening carefully to the argument as presented by Uncle Alec, Charlene Butterwick, Odelia, and Chase. Along with our humans, we had also been allowed to travel along. But even though our presence had been found acceptable, we had been relegated to the corner of the office, where we were being kept company by Mac and Cheese, the President's Dobermanns whom we had met on a previous occasion. The fact that our Hampton Cove delegation had been granted an audience with the President was thanks to the fact that we had saved the man's life not that long ago, and he still remembered.

"So how's life been treating you, fellas?" asked Mac. Once upon a time, he and his canine friend hadn't been pleased to make our acquaintance, but their initial hostility had quickly been replaced with gratitude for saving their human, and the old kinship still remained.

"Oh, we can't complain," I said.

"I have been poisoned with bug spray," said Harriet

apropos of nothing. "But I survived. And now I'm Santa's little helper, saving pets from being abused by their pet parents."

"Is that a fact?" asked Cheese with an indulgent smile. "Well, you don't have to bother about saving us. We're being treated very well by the President and his family. In fact, life couldn't be better for us, isn't that right, Mac?"

"Yeah, things are going swimmingly," said his friend. I hadn't been able to determine whether they were brothers or merely looked similar, and I was afraid to ask. They towered over us, and even though they were predisposed to be friendly to us, there was still an innate sense of danger that lurked underneath the surface and could be unleashed at any time.

The President leaned forward. "Okay, so what you're saying is that this man, this…"

"Rogelio Hartshorn," said Uncle Alec helpfully.

"That his life is effectively in danger and that these people will keep on coming until he's dead?"

"That's right," said the chief.

"But why? Why do they want him dead so much?"

"Well, the Abou-Yamens feel that he's been instrumental in assisting Prince Abdullah make certain claims that they have denied him."

"You see, Prince Abdullah fell out of favor with his grandfather, the king of Abou-Yamen," said Odelia, "when he imported a bug spray that didn't have the effect that it should have had. Instead of killing the bugs that were attacking their crops, the bugs proliferated, and the harvest failed, leading to a very difficult period and even what can only be called a famine. And so Prince Abdullah was deemed responsible and considered persona non grata. He was exiled and disinherited. If he had stayed in the country he would have been imprisoned."

"Prince Abdullah is the man that was killed in your town, isn't he?" asked the President.

"He is," said Odelia. "We believe that he was murdered on behalf of the Abou-Yamen government after he had begun a procedure to have his disinheritance retracted. He had hired Rogelio Hartshorn to plead his case and had also restarted negotiations with the same people who had provided the flawed bug spray and was going to have more of the stuff imported into Abou-Yamen to prove that he was right and his grandfather was wrong. This angered the king so much that he ordered to have his grandson killed and the murder pinned on the people selling the bug spray, Carlos Perks and Mindy Horsefield. He also ordered to have Rogelio Hartshorn killed as well. But in the end, only Prince Abdullah died."

"And you think they'll keep coming back to get rid of the lawyer and also the bug spray people?"

"Yes, once the king has issued an order it cannot be revoked. It has to be carried out, so they will keep trying to get rid of these people—all three of them American citizens, Mr. President."

"Hmm," said the president. "Tough case."

"So we were hoping that you could put some pressure on the Abou-Yamen government to have the kill order revoked," said Chase. "And save the lives of Rogelio Hartshorn, Carlos Perks and Mindy Horsefield."

"They're in hiding at the moment?"

"Carlos Perks and Mindy Horsefield are in prison right now awaiting trial," said Uncle Alec. "Not only did they make false claims about their bug spray and sold the stuff without FDA approval, but they recently launched themselves in the pet food business as well and there have been some complaints about their line of products."

"Carlos Perks is a chemist," said Odelia. "And he likes to

experiment. Unfortunately his experiments have a habit of going south. He's like a sorcerer's apprentice in that sense."

"They're selling bad pet food?" asked the President, darting a worried glance at his dogs.

"They sell one type of kibble but package it in different bags and sell it at different price points. But basically it's the exact same stuff—and pretty low quality, too. Junk food for pets."

"I see," said the president, rubbing his square chin. "Well, I will certainly talk to the Secretary of State. He'll have to lead the negotiations with his Abou-Yamen counterpart. And if that doesn't work, I'll pick up the phone and talk to the king of Abou-Yamen myself and tell him in no uncertain terms how I feel about him assassinating Americans on American soil."

"Thank you, Mr. President," said Charlene. "Mr. Hartshorn has been staying at my house for the time being, but he's eager to return home and go on with his life. He didn't ask for this."

"No, I certainly appreciate that. And I want to thank you for having the courage to come all the way to Washington to bring this matter to my attention. Not everyone would have gone to these lengths to help these people. It just shows that you all have your hearts in the right place and want to do the right thing. And I can tell you right now that I will do the same." He got up and buttoned up his jacket. "I will keep you posted, of course." He then saw that Mac and Cheese were engaged in pleasant conversation with the four of us and smiled. "So nice to see those kitties get along so well with my boys. They seem to remember each other from last time."

"I'm sure they do, Mr. President," said Odelia.

"I always wanted cats, you know, but my wife prefers dogs. And so do the kids. And Mac and Cheese haven't disappointed. They're the loveliest pair of mutts around. They spend more time in this office than I do!"

They all laughed politely at the President's little joke, and then it was time to go. He assured us that he would take the matter up with the king of Abou-Yamen, and that there would be no more killings of innocent people—though in the case of Carlos and Mindy, their innocence had yet to be determined. But then adulterating pet kibble and selling bad bug spray doesn't carry the death sentence. Otherwise, a lot of people would be on death row right now.

We said our goodbyes to Mac and Cheese and got ready to make the long trek home from Washington D.C. to Long Island. We all felt that the trip hadn't been in vain, and the atmosphere in the car was jubilant to a degree.

But then all of a sudden Harriet produced a tiny burp, and for some reason a bubble emerged from between her lips.

Odelia turned around in alarm. "Who was that?"

"Me," said Harriet, and produced another burp and another bubble. And as we watched in horror and surprise, she started hiccupping a storm, and a series of bubbles emerged from her lips. Before long, she looked like one of those bubble machines that are a big hit at kids' parties.

Odelia's lips turned into a thin line and she growled, "When I get my hands on Gran I'm going to kill her!"

Looked like the President would have to extend his executive powers to prevent murder and mayhem of American citizens on domestic soil to Grandma Muffin!

CHAPTER 36

Harriet wasn't feeling very well, but being the brave trooper that she was, she soldiered on in the face of this latest calamity that had befallen her. She was, after all, a diva, and any diva worth her salt doesn't allow a slight hiccup in the form of some medical malady to stop her from doing what she does best: to shine and to give people their money's worth!

And so after they had paid a visit to the President in his white house, and in spite of the fact that she had suddenly turned into a bubble machine, she wanted to give vent to her satisfaction with the way the case had been handled by singing a song. So she asked Brutus to pick a tune, and he selected *It's All Coming Back to Me Now* by Celine Dion. An excellent choice, and one of her personal favorites. And so she collected herself for a moment, closed her eyes, took a deep breath—diaphragm, diaphragm, diaphragm!—and… produced more bubbles!

Instead of Celine's wonderful song, out came bubbles and more bubbles, and as they popped, oddly enough, sound seemed to erupt from them. A bubble flew against Odelia's head and as it popped a note was heard. More bubbles floated through the car and popped and more notes were heard. All in all, it was quite the spectacle, and as those inhabiting the car expressed their surprise, she felt that maybe she had just invented a new genre: the bubble song!

"Shoot a video!" she urged between two bubbles. "Odelia, quick!"

Odelia did as she was told, and as Harriet sang more of the inimitable Miss Celine's big hit, the bubble musical festival continued unabated.

At the end, she smiled contentedly. When Odelia posted this video, she had good reason to suspect it would go viral and cement her reputation as America's foremost feline soprano. Fame and fortune awaited her! Now if only she could get rid of this hiccup and these bubbles! Though maybe she shouldn't wish to be cured. Maybe this would be the hallmark of her art. Maybe a year from now she would be performing her bubble songs in Madison Square Garden!

As she harbored this roseate dream, she finally fell asleep. It had, after all, been a long day.

* * *

WE WATCHED as our friend finally found sleep. From time to time, little bubbles escaped her lips and her nostrils, and I wondered how she could sleep while having been turned into a feline bubble machine, but then she was probably so exhausted after everything that had happened that nothing could keep her from visiting the land of dreams.

"I'm worried about her, Max," Brutus confessed. "Now with this bubble business. Are these strange side effects going to go away or is this just the harbinger of worse things to come?"

"No idea," I confessed. "But I have a feeling that gradually she will return to normal."

We had no way of knowing what Carlos Perks had put in his bug spray. If it had indeed been instrumental in causing a famine in Prince Abdullah's home country of Abou-Yamen, it didn't bode well for the future of anyone who had been in contact with the stuff. But since we had accepted that Vena Aleman might not be the terrible monster that we had always taken her for, we hoped she would be able to find a solution for Harriet's ailments, many as they were.

"Do you think the President will be able to stop Rogelio from being shot?" asked Brutus.

"I'm sure he will," I said. "You can't go around murdering people in other countries without facing some kind of blowback. I think they were hoping to get away with it. That nobody would find out. But now that their plan has been exposed, most likely they will back down. They don't want to face international criticism over this business with the prince."

"At least they didn't put a contract out on our lives," said Brutus with a shiver.

"Now why would they go and do that? We didn't have anything to do with the bug spray disaster."

"No, but we were instrumental in stopping the attacks on Rogelio, their sworn enemy," said Brutus. "So they might figure that as we stand in the way of the happy ending, they should take care of us first before they can get to Rogelio and Carlos and Mindy."

"I doubt it," I said. "They're not going to start murdering people willy-nilly. I think they'll suffice with the promise that Carlos and Mindy will face serious consequences for their actions, and since Prince Abdullah is no longer with us, they'll consider the problem dealt with and the threat eliminated."

"Good," said Brutus. He glanced over at Dooley, who seemed to be ruminating on something. "Everything all right with you, buddy?" he asked.

"Oh, I'm fine," Dooley assured him. "Just thinking about Rogelio, you know. And how if Max hadn't figured it out, that hotel manager would have shot him. Good thing we were there to stop it from happening."

"Yeah, I guess Rogelio is lucky to be alive," I said.

Dooley turned to me. "Max?"

"Yes, buddy?"

"Can you do me one big favor?"

"Sure. What is it?"

"Next time when you have a brainwave like that, can you take me through it?"

"What do you mean, take you through it? Take you through what?"

"Your brainwave. I would like to have brainwaves like that myself, you see. So if you can take me through it, I'll know how it works, and then next time I can have my own brainwave. I think it would be good for there to be more than one pet detective in town, you know."

"Sure thing," I said. I didn't know if explaining my thought process would help Dooley in any way, but if it made him happy I was certainly prepared to go into the details—if I could. Brainwaves are tricky things. It's not always easy to catch them and explain how they work.

"I mean, Harriet and Brutus are Santa's little helpers now, and you're a famous pet detective. So where does that leave me, you know?"

"You're my loyal assistant," I said. "My sidekick."

He smiled. "Yeah, I guess that's true. I am your sidekick, aren't I? The cat that makes it all happen."

"Absolutely. How else do you think I get these brainwaves if not because of you?"

"Someone has to provide the spark, Dooley," Brutus explained. "Without a spark, nothing happens. And you're the spark. So in a sense you could say that you're the most important part of this whole process—the most important member of our team."

Dooley teared up a little at that. "Gee, thanks, Brutus," he sniffed. "I've never looked at it that way. I *am* the spark—the spark that sets off Max's big brain. Without me, there's nothing."

"Exactly," said Brutus, giving me a wink. "And don't you forget it, buddy. Cause we're all counting on you."

CHAPTER 37

Tex had hauled the barbecue set out of storage and was happily dumping coals and accelerator fluid on the thing before using a spark to light it up, not unlike the way Dooley provided the spark that lit up my brain—if Brutus's theory was anything to go by. In actual fact, anything could provide the spark that set my thought process in motion. Something I saw, heard, or read about. It was all grist for the mill, and since I couldn't explain exactly how it worked, I didn't even try. It's not an exact science, and it would be hard for me to codify. For now, I was happy my brain was still capable of figuring things out and being of service.

Odelia seemed happy that the case had been put to bed, and so was the rest of the family. Charlene and Uncle Alec were happy that their guest had been able to return home after they had received word from the President's office that the king of Abou-Yamen had promised that Rogelio was safe, and also the couple he held responsible for the famine that had ravaged his country. Carlos and Mindy would have to stand trial for their transgressions, one of the king's demands in exchange for his promise that he wouldn't try to get rid of them anymore.

Harriet had mostly stopped bubbling, though from time to time tiny bubbles still emerged from her ears. Vena had told Odelia that as far as she could tell, Harriet was fine and wouldn't suffer any adverse effects from the insecticide Gran had subjected her to. The product itself had been removed from the shelves of every shop in the country after the video of Harriet had gone viral, as she had hoped. But instead of showcasing her talent as a singer, it had served as a warning. In other words, she had become a hero of the PSA, not the next Beyoncé. She still seemed satisfied that her likeness was being spread all across the country as the bubbling cat.

"Fame is fame, Max!" she told me. "It doesn't matter what you're famous for, as long as you're famous."

I could have told her that some celebrities are famous for being terrible people, and I wasn't sure that was the way to go. But in her case, there was no chance of that. Harriet may be a diva, and a little too much to handle from time to time, but she is essentially a sweetheart and our dear, dear friend—and we all love her to pieces—bubbles or no bubbles. And in her new capacity as Santa's little helper she had been instrumental in giving Vena's pet gerbil Jevon some respite from his cage, with Vena promising to let him out more often, and also to get her kids to take a break from their video games and instead play with their pet a little more.

In other words: Harriet was in the business of spreading sweetness and light—and bubbles.

I rubbed my paws in happy anticipation as Tex started doling out those delicious nuggets to keep the party going, and as our humans all dug in and we savored the smell of the nice goodies we had been given, for a moment, nobody spoke as our stomachs kept us occupied.

"Okay, I have to ask this," said Charlene, addressing Scarlett. "How do you do it, Scarlett?"

"Do what?" asked Scarlett as she daintily pronged a piece of chicken and took a bite.

"Looking as good as you do! What's your secret?"

Scarlett smiled, and I got the impression it wasn't the first time anyone had asked this question. "It's all about moisturizing. You have got to keep moisturizing, Charlene, honey."

"But I do moisturize," said Charlene, "and still I don't look half as good as you do, and I'm thirty years younger."

"You're probably doing it wrong," said Scarlett. "Do you rub your face cream?"

"Sure. Rub it in so it is absorbed by the skin."

"Well, you shouldn't. You have to dab it on." She demonstrated by placing her index and middle finger on her face. "See? Dab dab dab. Don't rub. Dab. That's the secret."

"Dab," said Charlene, nodding. "I'll keep it in mind."

"Should we also moisturize, Max?" asked Dooley. "So we look as good as Scarlett does?"

I smiled. "Even if we get wrinkles, nobody will notice, because we've got all of that fur, see?"

"Maybe that's the solution for Charlene," said Harriet. "Maybe she should grow fur on her face, then nobody will notice if she ages or not."

"There are creams that make hair grow in odd places," said Brutus.

"Maybe we should replace Charlene's face cream with one of those," said Harriet. "I'm sure she would be delighted."

"Yeah, I'm sure she would," I murmured. I could just imagine Charlene's surprise when she woke up one morning to find her face covered in fur. She would not be happy.

"I dab all the time," said Gran. "I'm an avid dabber. Always have been. And look at me. My face got more crevices than the Grand Canyon. So I call bullshit on your secret, Scarlett."

"You're probably not doing it right," said Scarlett. "Here, let me show you." She dug into her purse and took out a little tub of cream. "Demonstrate for me," she said as she handed the little tub to her friend.

Gran shrugged and unscrewed the lid and dug her fingers in, taking a big wad of the stuff.

"That's way too much!" Scarlett cried.

"I always put this much cream on my face," said Gran.

"Well, it's too much. Put some of it back. Put it back! Do you know how much this costs? It's the same stuff Kylie Jenner rubs on her face!"

Gran put some of the stuff back and used the rest to start dabbing at her face.

"That's not dabbing, that's slapping," said Scarlett. "You're punishing your face!"

"How else is this cream going to go in?" asked Gran. "You have to drive it home!"

"You have to be gentle. Like a caress. Here, let me show you." And she took a little bit of cream and started ever so gently dabbing it at her face. "Like an angel's wings," she explained.

"It's gonna take forever that way," Gran grumbled.

"It does take time," Scarlett admitted. "But it's worth it."

"How long does your morning skincare routine last?" asked Charlene.

"Oh, about two hours?" said Scarlett.

Charlene gulped, Vesta's jaw dropped, Marge goggled at the woman, and Odelia laughed.

"Crazy," Gran determined as she shook her head and handed back the cream to her friend.

"If you want to look good, you have to put in the time. There's no other way."

"I don't have that kind of time," said Charlene.

"And nor do you need it, sweetheart," said Uncle Alec as he pressed a kiss to her cheek. "You're beautiful as you are."

Charlene didn't look convinced. "Maybe I should start getting up earlier," she said.

"Me too," said Marge. She turned to Scarlett. "Could you demonstrate your routine to me in detail? I would like to know how it works, exactly."

"Of course. Why don't I organize a girl's night, and we can talk skincare all night long."

"That sounds great," said Charlene, looking much relieved.

"Exactly what I need," said Odelia.

"But honey, your skin is perfect!" said Marge.

"Not so perfect," said Odelia. "I found a blemish yesterday. Two blemishes, in fact."

"I also found a blemish," said Grace. "So count me in. You can't start early enough," she said when she found me staring at her.

"Oh, boy," said Brutus. "Am I glad I'm not a human. Two hours to apply cream to your face in the morning, and maybe two hours at night to take it off again? What a drag."

It certainly sounded like something I wouldn't want to do. But then I guess humans are a little weird. They want to keep looking good until the moment they pass to the great beyond and will do anything to accomplish that. And more power to them. After all, it's good to have goals in life. Aspirations. And if your aspiration is to look good, that's fine with me.

"Do you think we should also spend two hours in the morning trying to look good, Max?" asked Dooley.

"I think cats have the advantage of looking good whatever they do, buddy," I said.

"We're gorgeous out of the box," said Harriet. "It's the way nature intended us to be." She burped and a tiny bubble escaped her lips. "Oops," she murmured.

"What do *you* do about skincare?" asked Uncle Alec.

"Me? Nothing," said Chase.

"No lotions, creams, nothing?"

"Nope. Nothing at all."

"Charlene has suggested I use a moisturizer," said the chief. "She says I have dry flaky skin."

"Not me," said Chase. "My skin is flawless."

"Lucky you," said the chief with a touch of envy.

"It's genetics. Nothing you can do about it. You can rub gallons of cream on your face and it won't make one bit of difference. Scarlett won the DNA lottery, that's all there is to it."

"Better don't tell that to Charlene," said the chief. "She's been on a cream binge lately, scouring the internet for the right cream to use on her skin and going through tons of the stuff."

"Won't help," said Chase -. "Either you got great skin or you don't."

"If you say so," said the chief, looking a little disappointed.

"What you need is a whiff of this," said Gran, and took out a can that looked very familiar. And then I recognized it: it was that same bug spray she had used on Harriet! She proceeded to spritz some of it on her son and Chase, who sat there looking quite shocked.

"Did you just use bug spray on us?" asked the chief.

"It's not bug spray," said Gran. "It's…" Then she checked the can. "Oh, shoot, you're right. It *is* bug spray. Strange. I thought I'd gotten rid of the stuff." She shrugged. "Oh, well."

The chief and Chase both turned a little green around the nostrils, and as they got up, both looked faint. Bubbles were escaping their mouths and as they made a run for the house,

I had a feeling that same nausea that had attacked Harriet now held them in its grip.

"What's wrong with Chase and Alec?" asked Charlene.

"Oh, nothing," said Gran as she quickly threw the can of spray under her chair. "Probably something to do with a case. I could have sworn that was hairspray," she whispered to Scarlett.

"Why would you use hairspray on their faces?" Scarlett whispered back.

"I read online that hairspray is the secret to great skin."

"Oh, Vesta," said Scarlett with a sigh.

Dooley directed a look of concern at the house. "Do you think Uncle Alec and Chase will be fine? They both looked sick."

"It's just a little bug spray," said Harriet. "They'll live." She produced another bubble. "Okay, so now you have to tell us all about the case, Max. This hotel manager. What was that all about, huh? Shouldn't a hotel manager take care of his guests, not murder them?"

"Yeah, killing guests is not in the job description," said Brutus.

"In the case of Garland McNerlin," I said, "it wasn't in his job description either. But apparently the man suffered from a serious gambling addiction and had accumulated a large debt that he couldn't possibly pay off unless he sold the hotel, which he didn't want to do. Remember the overdue bills piling up on his desk? The man was in debt up to his ears. And so the people he owed money to suggested a way of making his problems go away and put him in touch with the Abou-Yamen secret service, who were looking for a way to get rid of Prince Abdullah, whom they blamed for the calamity that had befallen their country."

"And so Garland shot the prince?" asked Harriet.

"He did, yeah. To gain access to the prince's room was a

cinch for him as he could print a key card and not make it show up on the database. He also tampered with the CCTV by removing the crucial minutes he was in the prince's room from the footage. All in all he perpetrated the perfect crime. And to top it off he placed the blame on the hapless bug spray people, with whom the Abou-Yamens also had a score to settle. Two birds killed in one stone."

"And Rogelio?" asked Dooley. "Why did they try and kill that nice Rogelio?"

"Because Prince Abdullah wanted his inheritance back, and his rightful position in the monarchy. And so he was going to fight for his right to inherit, with Rogelio in his corner."

"And the Abou-Yamens couldn't have that?" asked Harriet.

"I think Prince Abdullah had created such a mess that the mere mention of his name caused the king of Abou-Yamen to have apoplexy. He hated his grandson so much he wanted him gone in the worst way possible, and every person associated with him."

"Poor Rogelio. He should never have taken the prince's call."

"So Marjorie Collett?" said Brutus.

"Doesn't exist," I said.

"But how did you find out, Max?" asked Harriet.

"Yes, tell us all about that brainwave, Max," said Dooley.

"I think the spark was the sausage," I said.

Dooley seemed disappointed. "I thought the spark was me?"

"Well, you and the sausage," I amended.

"I don't get it," said Brutus. "What sausage? What are you talking about?"

"Remember Norm's friend the cockroach? He said the prince had dropped a piece of pork sausage on the floor. But in Abou-Yamen pork is strictly forbidden. It told me that Prince Abdullah was a bad boy who didn't like to follow the rules of his country too closely. And then there was the fact that he had been caught pickpocketing from the General Store. To me that painted a picture of a royal who was off the reservation. And then there was that message written on the prince's bathroom mirror. 'You'll pay for this.' Which made me wonder if there was a connection between the famine that had hit Abou-Yamen and the bug spray the prince had imported. Chase made a couple of calls and discovered that Prince Abdullah had been disinherited by his grandfather and kicked out of the country. He was persona non grata."

"Poor prince," said Dooley feelingly. "To be kicked out of the country by his own family."

"And being murdered by his own family," Brutus pointed out.

"There were probably other transgressions that we will never know about," I said. "Suffice it to say that the royal house of Abou-Yamen felt that Prince Abdullah had disgraced them. And so he had to die. And who better to task with the murder than a hotel manager in debt?"

"And two not-too-bright crooks," Brutus added. "To get rid of the prince's lawyer."

"It didn't hurt that Garland McNerlin is an ex-marine," I said. Something else Chase's investigation had discovered. It certainly explained the man's proficiency with firearms.

"I still think it's all very sad," Dooley insisted. "Just because the prince liked to eat sausage from time to time…"

"And caused a famine in his country," I pointed out. "And did who knows what else."

"Still. They could have forgiven him and allowed him to return to the bosom of the family. The prodigal son, you know." He sighed. "Everybody loves a bad boy, don't they?"

"Not the people of Abou-Yamen, apparently."

Tex supplied us with some more tasty grub, and smiled when he saw the reception his creations were receiving. "I'll go and make some more," he promised.

Chase and Uncle Alec had returned from their urgent visit to the bathroom. They still looked a little green around the gills, and their appetite seemed to have taken a hit. We didn't mind. It just meant there was more for the rest of us. And judging from Harriet, apart from some bubble action, they would soon be right as rain again. After all, it isn't just us who have to suffer when Gran gets some bee in her bonnet. Both the benefits and the drawbacks of living with a woman like Vesta Muffin should be spread fairly amongst her nearest and dearest.

Just then, Norm settled on the swing next to me. He looked complacent, I thought.

"It's done," he announced. "One hundred kiddies, waiting to hatch."

"Hatch?" I asked.

"Yeah, they're in the larval state now. Soon they'll become pupae and then they hatch." He sighed happily. "Oh, you guys, it's such a great feeling to be a dad! There's nothing like it!"

"Where... where did Norma deposit these larvae of hers?" I asked, suddenly getting an awful suspicion. One hundred larvae had to feed, didn't they? And they were clearly somewhere nearby, or Norm wouldn't be sitting there chatting with us.

"Like I told you, she found a great place," said Norm.

"But... where exactly is this great place?"

He vaguely pointed in the direction of the garden house. "Norma found us a good spot right over there. Plenty of high-quality nosh to tide the little ones over until they hatch."

It suddenly dawned on me that Marge keeps a nice stash

of our food in that garden house. Several bags, in fact, for safe storage. "High-quality nosh?"

"Yeah, bags and bags of the stuff. I don't know who put it there but Norma and I are very grateful. There's enough food to feed an army." He laughed happily. "An army of flies!"

I slapped my brow. Looked like our 'great nosh' would soon be crawling with maggots!

"Okay, much as I enjoy these conversations, I have to be off," said Norm. "Norma wants to go for another batch." He grinned. "Better keep my strength up, you guys." And with this, he settled on the pork chop that Tex had dropped in my bowl, dribbled some saliva on it, and sucked the liquified piece of pork chop into his mouth. Then he was off, to make more flies!

Brutus and I shared a look. "No good deed goes unpunished, Max," he said.

And ain't that the truth.

THE END

Thanks for reading! If you want to know when a new Nic Saint book comes out, sign up for Nic's mailing list: nicsaint.com/news

EXCERPT FROM PURRFECT HEIST (MAX 89)

Chapter One

Dooley had been keeping a close eye on his human for the last couple of days, and when he saw her traipsing through Blake's Field in her underwear, he knew that his concerns had been justified all along. Even his best friend Max had told him that he was exaggerating and that Gran was fine. Obviously she wasn't fine. She was anything but fine. But since Max was home, he couldn't tell him that he had been right and that Max was wrong. Not that he would have done so, since that wasn't Dooley's style.

He followed Gran from a little distance, making sure she didn't notice she was being followed. She wouldn't have liked it since she was a proud old lady and wouldn't have condoned a chaperone in the form of her own kitty. He wondered where she was going and why she would venture out of the house in the middle of the night, only dressed in her undies. The situation was certainly cause for grave concern. He followed her all the way to the small derelict shack that was still located on the field and hadn't been taken

EXCERPT FROM PURRFECT HEIST (MAX 89)

down, even though the entire neighborhood had asked the field's owner many times.

He watched from a safe distance as Gran took a seat in front of the shack, on a crooked bench that had seen better days, and folded her hands in her lap, sitting prim and proper. Then she reached into her pocket and took out a bag containing something he couldn't quite make out. She reached into the bag, and the next moment started singing softly to herself. *"Feed the birds,"* she sang. *"Feed the birds. Tuppence a bag. Tuppence a bag."* And as he watched on in amazement and a rising sense of concern, she started strewing breadcrumbs from the bag. But since it was the middle of the night, there weren't any birds present to partake in this moderate feast. Instead, a couple of the mice that lived in the old shack emerged from their hiding places, sniffed the air for a moment, and then descended on the breadcrumbs, gobbling them up with relish.

So now Gran had taken to feeding the mice? But why? He simply didn't understand what was going on, except that he should probably tell somebody before one of the neighbors noticed Gran's strange behavior and had her locked up in an institution.

He wondered for a moment if he shouldn't approach the old lady and tell her to go back to bed. He had been lying at the foot of her bed when she had ventured out, but when he had asked her where she thought she was going, she hadn't replied, but had simply slipped her feet into her slippers and had left the house. And since he didn't want her to get into trouble, he had decided to follow her and see where she was going.

As he watched, she crumpled up the bag and put it back into her pocket, then rocked back and forth for a moment, humming the same tune under her breath, a happy smile on

EXCERPT FROM PURRFECT HEIST (MAX 89)

her face. She was staring before her, seemingly looking at nothing in particular.

The mice had dispensed with the last pieces of bread and returned to their nest to deliver the good news that a new benefactor was in town and that they might be looking forward to many more nights like this, with Gran delivering food to their little home.

Dooley knew the mice since he had made their acquaintance on several occasions, and he could only applaud their good fortune. It still didn't allay his general sense of unease at this type of behavior from one who he had always admired and loved.

He now wondered if he should tell Marge that her mother had developed this strange new habit of feeding the mice. Marge would worry, of course, since she was that kind of person. But that couldn't be helped. At least she would tell Tex, and the doctor could take a closer look at the strange behavior his mother-in-law had started displaying lately.

For this wasn't the first time Gran had ventured out like this, though mostly she had limited her nocturnal sojourn to the backyard. This was the first time she had ventured out beyond the perimeter of her own home. If this kept up, pretty soon she would start wandering all over Hampton Cove, or even the entire island or maybe the state.

As he watched on, he saw that a dark figure had appeared, hiding behind a nearby tree. The dark figure was watching Gran, biding his time. Dooley's heart jumped into his throat when he realized that his human might be in some kind of grave danger.

Gran hadn't noticed the dark figure, but then she wasn't in a state to notice much of anything right now. He wondered if he should warn her that she was being watched.

Then again, it might be one of the neighbors walking their

EXCERPT FROM PURRFECT HEIST (MAX 89)

dog in the middle of the night and wondering what Gran was up to. They could be excused for wanting to know what was going on—the same way Dooley wanted to know what she was up to.

He saw that the figure detached themselves from that tree and approached Gran. He still couldn't make out their face or other distinguishing features, but it was clear that the figure was just as curious to find out what was going on as he himself was.

The figure walked right up to Gran and stood before her. Gran still didn't react in any meaningful way, and that's when Dooley understood: she was sleepwalking!

He had heard about this kind of behavior, where people get out of bed in the middle of the night and do all kinds of stuff that they later don't remember. It was not a good thing, especially since she was away from home and vulnerable, as the situation showed.

His words of warning were stuck in his throat, or he would have called out to Gran to wake up and get out of there. For the person had taken out what looked like a great big knife and now stood wielding it in front of Gran's face. The old lady was still smiling and didn't seem to notice what was going on.

The figure must have realized that she formed no threat whatsoever, for he or she put the knife away again, waved a hand in front of Gran's eyes, then shrugged and took off.

Dooley breathed a sigh of relief, and even more so when Gran finally got up and started on the short trek home.

It wasn't long before she was crawling back into bed and dragging the covers over her ears. Dooley eyed her for a few moments from his vantage point at the foot of the bed. But when he heard his human's slow and even breathing, he finally lay down his head and slept.

Tomorrow he would tell Marge. Clearly, something had to be done.

EXCERPT FROM PURRFECT HEIST (MAX 89)

Chapter Two

Kurt Mayfield was walking his dog Fifi and wondering not for the first time if his time couldn't be better spent some other, more productive, way. After all, Fifi had the use of the entire backyard, and if she wanted to, even the field behind the house, though he normally didn't condone that she snuck underneath the fence.

Still, dogs needed to be walked, or so common sense dictated. And it was true that there was an added benefit in that he got to satisfy one of his secret pastimes: spying on his neighbors. Nobody appreciated it when you blatantly took up position in front of their homes and stared into their living rooms and watched what they did. But when you held a dog on the leash, it was accepted behavior. What he didn't like about dog walking was that you ran the risk of bumping into other dog walkers, and invariably they would engage him in conversation, asking questions about this or that, generally making a nuisance of themselves. This is why he had adopted the practice of walking Fifi very early in the morning, at six o'clock, and late at night, just before he went to bed. That way, the risk of running into his neighboring blabbermouths was a lot less. Some of them had even started a WhatsApp group and arranged to walk their dogs together. To Kurt, that was what hell must be like. He had kindly declined to be added to the group.

Gilda, his neighbor and also his girlfriend, often told him he was a curmudgeon, and she probably had a point. But then after sixty-eight years of being a grouch, what were the chances that he would ever change? Once a grouch, always a grouch, and he riposted by telling her that she seemed to like him anyway, to which she admitted this was true.

"I have tamed the grouch of Harrington Street," she said

EXCERPT FROM PURRFECT HEIST (MAX 89)

laughingly. "And I should probably deserve some kind of prize."

Funny girl.

He passed by Blake's Field and Fifi, as was her habit, yanked and strained at the leash to take a peek inside their local jungle. Years of neglect had turned the field into a haven of weeds and trees and shrubs, and if he had complained to the town council once, he had complained a million times. Ownership of the field was in some kind of legal limbo at the moment, and as long as the lawyers representing the previous owners and the town council didn't get their act together and turn it into something that was a boon to the neighborhood instead of an eyesore, there was nothing anyone could do about it.

At least it wasn't a big building pit, for once upon a time there had been plans to develop the land, which would have been imminently worse if it had gone through.

"All right, all right," he said as Fifi barked up a storm. "I'll bite." Probably she wanted to take a look at that old shack, which seemed to hold a special appeal to the little Yorkie. Once upon a time she had even found a dead body there. It had been quite the scandal. A murder, in a pleasant neighborhood like theirs? Absolutely unheard of.

He hurried after Fifi, hoping he didn't step into something nasty. Since he wasn't the only dog owner who used Blake's Field to allow their beloved mutts some off-leash time, the grass had been trampled on and flattened and a natural sort of pathway had formed that led from the street to the shack. He could have followed it with his eyes closed since he had walked this same route many times with Fifi.

She barked happily when they finally reached the old shack, and the moment he unleashed her, she started prancing around and happily jumping up against his legs.

He smiled and affectionately patted her on the head.

EXCERPT FROM PURRFECT HEIST (MAX 89)

"Go on, girl," he said encouragingly. "You go on."

This was her time, and she knew it.

He took a seat on the bench that had been placed in front of the shack and watched as his little doggie disappeared into the high weeds that surrounded the shack. From time to time he saw her jumping up, her head briefly clearing the weeds and shrubs, then she was gone again, possibly chasing a rabbit or some other creature of the undergrowth.

The shack itself was home to a colony of mice, and he suspected there were also plenty of rats and other vermin housed there. From time to time a chicken would pop its head up. They used to belong to Ted Trapper but had escaped captivity and were now roaming wild and free, just like all the other creatures that occupied this plot of land.

He didn't mind, as long as they didn't cross the boundary with his backyard and enter his private property. Even the vermin of this world should know its place.

He glanced around, and when he didn't see anyone, took a small silver case out of his jacket pocket, extracted a cigarette, and lit one up. As he took a long drag, he closed his eyes with relish and directed a plume of smoke at the sky. Gilda had told him that smoking was a filthy habit, and to accommodate her, he had cut down to two ciggies a day: one during each time he took Fifi for her walks. Another benefit of having a dog.

As he fixed his eyes on a point in the distance where he knew his house was located, he thought he saw something bright red hanging from a nearby tree. He frowned as he got up. As far as he could tell, he had never seen anything hanging from that tree before. Maybe another dog walker had accidentally left it behind? Or maybe kids had been playing there, even though most of the parents living on this block strictly forbade their offspring from venturing out there, since there were rumors that drug addicts used the

EXCERPT FROM PURRFECT HEIST (MAX 89)

shack to engage in their favorite pastime. In other words: not exactly a playground.

He walked up to the tree and saw that the red item was a sweater. He took it down and studied it. No name tag. It looked new and probably belonged to someone who was missing it now. He wondered if he should take it along to give to his neighbor Chase Kingsley. The cop could take it into the station with him and drop it off at the lost-and-found. As he folded up the sweater, something fell out of a hidden pocket. It was a piece of jewelry, and as he picked it up from the ground, he saw that it was a little golden cross. Very nice, he thought as he turned it over in his hand. And probably expensive. There were markings on the cross, but since he hadn't taken his reading glasses along with him, he couldn't quite make them out. He closed his fist around the little trinket and was more determined now to hand it over to Chase. He'd know what to do with it.

He returned to the bench to finish his smoke when he thought he saw movement in the shrubbery nearby. "Fifi?" he said. But it wasn't Fifi who emerged. It was a large person wearing a hoodie, which partially obscured his or her face. Before he could ask what they were doing there, the stranger took out a gun and pulled the trigger. Kurt felt a stinging pain in his chest, and as he went down, he thought that of all the things that could happen to a person walking his dog, the oddest had to be to get shot and killed.

Poor Fifi. Now what would become of her?

Chapter Three

I had been idly glancing out of the upstairs bedroom window when I thought I heard a loud bang. The kind of bang that only a gun can make. As it seemed to be coming from Blake's Field, I wondered if perhaps someone had taken

EXCERPT FROM PURRFECT HEIST (MAX 89)

advantage of the early hour to go and do some hunting. As everyone knows, there are plenty of rabbits that have made the field their home, and some people seem to enjoy rabbit meat as much as others like chicken or beef.

Next to me, my friend Dooley also looked up. "What was that?" he asked.

"Sounded like a gunshot," I said. "Coming from Blake's Field."

He shook his head. "I'm telling you, Max, ever since Gran started walking around in the middle of the night, I haven't slept a wink."

I could have told him this was a blatant lie, for I had seen him—and heard him—sleep a perfectly sound wink at the foot of Odelia's bed. Dooley likes to divide his time between my home and that belonging to Odelia's mom and dad. In other words, his loyalties are divided between his own human and Odelia, who is probably the more responsible of our pet parents. Though Odelia's mom, Marge, isn't too shabby either.

"I just hope that Gran hasn't been shot," said Dooley, as he gave me a look of alarm.

"If you like, we can go and take a look," I suggested. "Though it's probably kids playing with a toy gun."

I have to say that it had sounded like a real gun, though, and not a toy alternative, since they don't make that much noise. And since we didn't want to wake up our humans, we decided to take a look for ourselves before we alerted Odelia and Chase.

Next to the bed, a second smaller bed had been placed, where Grace slept. At one point, she would get her own bedroom, but for now, she still enjoyed sleeping in her parents' bedroom. The sound of the gunshot must also have awakened her, for she yawned and stretched. "What was that noise?" she asked.

EXCERPT FROM PURRFECT HEIST (MAX 89)

"We're not sure," I said. "But we think it was a gunshot."

"It was coming from Blake's Field," said Dooley.

"We're going to take a look," I added.

"I'll come with you," she said, and threw off her blanket.

"No, you're not," I said. "You will stay right here."

"But I want to come!" she insisted.

"It might be dangerous, Grace," I said.

"As long as I'm with you guys, there's no danger," she argued. "You will be my bodyguards, won't you?"

And since she is one of those people who likes to do as she says and do it now, she climbed down from her bed and padded in the direction of the door.

"At least wear some shoes," I said.

"And a coat!" Dooley added.

We hurried after her, and I wondered what else we could say to make her stay put. The last thing we needed was for Grace to get shot out there in Blake's Field. Even if it was just kids playing, the field definitely was not a place for her to hang out. She was too little and Dooley and I hardly qualified as bodyguards.

But since Grace does what Grace wants, we had no alternative but to follow her out of the house and then to the fence, where Chase has put a sort of stepladder to allow us to climb the fence and climb down the other side. He probably didn't think it would also give his daughter license to do the same thing. Without waiting for us to catch up, the little girl was already clambering over that fence with surprising agility, almost as if she had never done anything else her entire life.

"She's an expert climber, Max," said Dooley, admiration clear in his voice.

"I'll say," I said.

"No, I said," he said.

EXCERPT FROM PURRFECT HEIST (MAX 89)

"It's an expression, Dooley. It means I agree with what you just said."

"Oh, right," he said, and hurried up and over that fence to make sure that Grace wouldn't get into all kinds of trouble.

I brought up the rear as I often do. I'm one of the heavyweight cats of this world, you see. Some people call me fat, but I would argue that it's simple genetics and that I was born with big bones. With some effort, I also made it over the fence, and when I arrived on the other side, it took me a moment to locate my friend and Grace. They had already ventured deeper into the weeds, and when I finally caught up with them, I saw they had reached the clearing in the center of the field. A shack had been built there, with a car wreck located next to it. It's mostly home to several colonies of mice, and also a colony of shrews and even a colony of ants, but when I looked closer, I saw that it wasn't mice or shrews or ants that were crawling all over the place but a larger species of creature.

"Rats!" said Dooley with dismay. "Max, look, it's rats!"

"I can see, Dooley," I assured him. There were indeed plenty of rats, and as we ventured a little closer still, I saw they were all sitting around an object that was lying on the ground. It was the body of a man, and as we took a good look at the man, I saw that he was familiar to us. It was none other than our next-door neighbor Kurt Mayfield!

Next to his body, a little doggie sat. It was Fifi, our good friend the Yorkshire terrier. She looked absolutely devastated, and had one paw draped over her human's chest, and the other brought up to her face to wipe her tears.

"Max! Dooley!" she cried. "Someone shot Kurt!"

So that was the gunshot we had heard. It wasn't kids, or a hunter hunting rabbits. It was someone taking a shot at the retired music teacher!

The rats had fled the moment we arrived, and a good

EXCERPT FROM PURRFECT HEIST (MAX 89)

thing, too, for they might have considered Kurt a nice meal and could have started nibbling at him, which is not what you want when you've just been shot.

"The blood must have attracted them," I said, pointing to our neighbor's blood-soaked shirt.

"Is he still alive?" asked Grace, who had also toddled up to the man and seemed unsure how to proceed.

"He's alive," said Fifi. She gave me a pained look. "I wanted to come and get you, but I was afraid to leave him alone with these rats. They were very mean to me, Max. They said I shouldn't stand in the way of a nice snack. And they also said there was enough for all of us and I was being selfish for not wanting to share!"

"We'll go and get Odelia and Chase," I told her. "Come on, Grace. Time to leave."

"I'll stay here," said Fifi, "and guard him, shall I?"

"You do that," I said.

And so we hurried back the same way we had come, to wake up our humans and make sure Kurt got the help he needed.

"Is he dead, Max?" asked Grace. "It's just that I've never seen a dead man."

"And nor should you see one," I told her. "At your age all you should see are the dolls you like to play with."

I could have kicked myself for allowing Grace to tag along. Though I also knew there was absolutely no way I could have stopped her. In that sense she had inherited her mother's stubbornness. One day she would make a great reporter—or cop—or both, like Odelia.

"I hope he won't die, Max," said Dooley. "Fifi would be devastated if he died."

"All the more reason to make haste," I urged.

We slammed into the bedroom, me panting up a storm, and Dooley and Grace still as light on their feet as they had

EXCERPT FROM PURRFECT HEIST (MAX 89)

been when we set out. One advantage was that when I jumped up on Odelia's chest, she immediately was wide awake. I may not be the fastest cat on the block, but I'm the best at waking people up through the judicious application of the force of gravity.

"Max," she groaned sleepily. "How many times have I told you not to sit on my chest?"

"It's Kurt," I said, not wasting any more time. "He's been shot."

Immediately, she was wide awake, and sat up with a jerk. I fell to the floor and when she saw me, Dooley, and Grace looking up at her, she realized I wasn't kidding.

"Chase," she said urgently, as she elbowed her husband in the ribs. "Wake up. Kurt Mayfield has been shot."

It probably wasn't the best way to start our day. But it was a darn sight better than Kurt's start. I just hoped he would live. For Dooley was right: if he died, Fifi would be devastated.

ABOUT NIC

Nic has a background in political science and before being struck by the writing bug worked odd jobs around the world (including but not limited to massage therapist in Mexico, gardener in Italy, restaurant manager in India, and Berlitz teacher in Belgium).

When he's not writing he enjoys curling up with a good (comic) book, watching British crime dramas, French comedies or Nancy Meyers movies, sampling pastry (apple cake!), pasta and chocolate (preferably the dark variety), twisting himself into a pretzel doing morning yoga, going for a brisk walk, and spoiling his feline assistants Lily and Ricky.

He lives with his wife (and aforementioned cats) in a small village smack dab in the middle of absolutely nowhere and is probably writing his next 'Mysteries of Max' book right now.

www.nicsaint.com

Printed in Great Britain
by Amazon